Shi Anne McMillan was born in Lisburn, Northern Ireland.
She udied at Queen's University, Belfast and Manchester
Met opolitan University. Shirley-Anne wrote and performed with
Bel st-based arts group, Ikon, for several years. She currently lives
in S ith Down where she spends her time as a writer, schools
wo and mum.

A GOOD HIDING

SHIRLEY-ANNE
M^CMILLAN

ATOM

ATOM

First published in Great Britain in 2016 by Atom

1 3 5 7 9 10 8 6 4 2

A CIP catalogue record for this book
is available from the British Library.

ISBN 978-0-349-00251-4

Typeset in Garamond by M Rules
Printed and bound in Great Britain by
Clays Ltd, St Ives plc

Papers used by Atom are from well-managed forests
and other responsible sources.

MIX
Paper from
responsible sources
FSC
www.fsc.org   FSC® C104740

Atom
An imprint of
Little, Brown Book Group
Carmelite House
50 Victoria Embankment
London EC4Y 0DZ

An Hachette UK Company
www.hachette.co.uk

www.atombooks.co.uk

To Ana

Noli timere

1

Nollaig

When I woke up that morning there was a cloud shadow on the south face of Cave Hill that was shaped like an angel.

My alarm went off and I slammed my hand down hard on it and hoped that Dad hadn't heard. I waited for a second until I could hear the loud drone of his boozy snoring and then I pulled back one side of the curtains. It looked like an angel to me anyway. It had a lumpy triangular shaped body and two fanned-out wings. Like when you're a wee kid and you make your body into an angel picture by lying down in the snow and waving your arms and legs about. But the more I looked at the shadow the less it seemed like something special. Sometimes you're just too tired to imagine good things. And then the sun broke through the bruises of the sky and chased it away. It started to rain again and I closed the curtain.

Dad always sleeps until about lunchtime. He'll get up, forget to eat anything, pour himself a whiskey and put the telly on, just in time for some rubbish lunchtime quiz show or something. He wasn't always a waster. He used to drive the bus to school, which was good, because I always got there on time, and bad, because it meant I could never mitch off. Different now, of course. Sometimes I'd come home from school and he'd still be in bed, which was fine by me because it meant I didn't have to talk to him. I could get changed and go out. Some days I didn't have to watch him wasting his life at all.

I got out of bed and pulled on my freezing jeans. I was set to skip school that day but it meant an early start. Glen High is totally on-the-ball about kids mitching off. They normally catch up with you about 11:30 a.m. You might think there are no possible advantages to having an alcoholic da but actually there are. One of the main advantages was that it gave me an extra couple of hours of freedom on days when I couldn't face school. But on this particular day I had loads to do and even with the extra time I had to hurry. I found my bra and shirt under a towel and took a breath as I stopped and had a look around the room. Clothes on the floor, a dirty mug, a couple of books. It wasn't much to say goodbye to but it still felt a bit sad. It's not every day you leave home.

There wasn't a choice any more. I'd thought about leaving before, loads of times, but now I had to make a move. You can put up with a lot, I reckon, loads of people do, but then something will happen and you have to do something about it. It was going to mean being tough, really tough, forgetting about dreams and angel shadows and stupid romantic ideas. It was going to mean forgetting about Stephen.

I found my red boots and wound the laces around the hooks. Quicker to put on trainers but I wasn't going without my old boots. The blood rushed to my head as I bent over. I made a mental note to eat something.

Stephen was going to be so pissed off. But shut up, I couldn't think of him now. Most people wouldn't notice I was gone. *Most people*. That was the main thing. There wouldn't be any internet campaigns to bring me back. Even if Stephen wanted to, there'd be no one to email because he was the only one that cared. There's this thing that Ms Laker the Drama teacher used to say: 'If life gives you lemons, make lemonade.' It's meant to mean that if your life's crap then you should turn it into something brilliant instead. It's a stupid thing to say, though, because you need sugar to make lemonade and what if you haven't got any? So I had decided; my life was full of lemons and I had no sugar so the choice was either put up with mouldy old fruit or kill myself, or, option three, go and look somewhere else for something good – forget about the dumb lemons and the stupid things teachers say and find out if I can make things different on my own, somewhere else. But it would mean really on my own – no Dad, no friends with good intentions who might tout on me when things got tough. Just me.

I found my old backpack jammed down the side of the bed. Big enough to hold what I needed, but small enough that it wouldn't make people wonder where I was going. I sat on the bed and emptied it out: a bus receipt, half a packet of Chewits and 50p. I unwrapped one of the sweets. It was half melted and it stuck to the paper but I ate it anyway and chucked the rest in the bin with the bus ticket.

Here is what I put in my bag:

Twenty £10 notes (I'd been nicking one out of Dad's wallet every week for ages now, in case of emergencies, and this was an emergency. I shoved them into my wallet.)

Packet of chocolate biscuits

Tube of Pringles (I popped it open and ate three at once)

Three apples (for vitamins)

Two small bottles of Coke

A load of underwear, two t-shirts and my big green jumper

Phone (crap one, but I've had it for ages)

Personal CD player and headphones (my mum's. It just about still works. The buttons stick sometimes and the 'shuffle' button doesn't work. When you open it, the lid springs up quickly and when you close it you have to hold it down hard with two fingers to make it click shut. I can play music on my phone but I like to have Mum's CD player with me too. It's personal. If people were being honest about the music they liked and they wrote down all their favourite songs in a list, I reckon there wouldn't be two people whose list was the same. It's like fingerprints. And if you listen to someone else's list it's the closest you can be to them without them actually being there. So I stuffed the player in my bag even though there wasn't a lot of room left, and I took two of her CDs too.)

I was travelling light. As light as I could for someone in my position.

First thing: a letter. I hated doing it this way but I needed to be sure no one was going to follow me. I rooted around to find something to write on – the back of an old piece of GCSE coursework about deprived housing in our area.

Dear Dad

It was impossible to write. I opened the curtains again and looked at the hills, big and solitary on the horizon. Maybe Dad wouldn't survive on his own. But he was almost dead now anyway. A zombie dad. He never spoke in a normal way – it was always either incoherent muttering or yelling awful stuff – and only went out if he was going to the offy's. All he did was watch telly and empty his glass. A fat tear sploshed on the page in front of me and the words swam into a blur. I scrunched up the note, wiped my face with the bottom of my t-shirt and started again.

Dear Dad
  I have to go. You won't see me again so don't try looking.
Sort out the drinking, it's killing you.
  Nollaig

I read it back and it sounded cold. I didn't feel cold but I should have. He didn't deserve a note, the old bastard. I thought about just leaving without saying a thing. Just disappearing from his life. But I needed to leave something so he knew I'd gone on purpose. Last night's pleasant exchange played again in my head.

'You goin' out, Nollaig? Where to?' He said it like an accusation, like I was going to rob a house or something. He was on the sofa, his back to me as I passed by the living room door. He didn't even turn around.

'Just out.' Why should I tell him anyway? I was only going to the shop but I didn't feel like talking to him.

Suddenly he swung round and the empty bottle of whiskey he'd been nursing went flying past my head.

'Why don't you just fuck off, you wee hoor.'

He needed to know that it was my decision to leave, not his. I could imagine him reading the note and thinking, 'About bloody time.'

It would have to do. It felt hard to breathe, like if I screamed or something the thing blocking my throat might come out. I couldn't do that. I had to stay tough. But standing in front of the bathroom mirror I didn't feel tough. Because, despite running away from everyone and leaving everything behind, there was one thing I would have to carry with me, and I needed to make sure it was really there.

I held my breath and picked up the test which I'd left on the edge of the bath. There it was, the little blue line connecting what I'd imagined to how things really were. I knew it would be there but when I saw it I doubled over, just managing to lurch to the toilet bowl before throwing up. Great, now I had to flush. Dad stirred next door. He called out in a sleepy slur,

'Noll? Wha's goin' on?'

I used to have this dream when I was wee, a nightmare really, about being cornered by a monster that I couldn't see properly, I could only hear it snarling and see the light glinting off its teeth. Sometimes when Dad spoke, even when he was so drunk that I knew he couldn't do anything, it felt like his voice was so big and low that someday it might actually become a thing on its own and attack you. I wished I wasn't so afraid of him. It wasn't always like that. He used to be a normal dad, a normal person, the kind that drinks tea in the morning and might even eat some toast. But that seemed like a long time ago now.

'It's not the mornin' yet, Da. Go back to sleep.'

'Urgh.'

A typical response. I tiptoed towards his room listening to the slow, rhythmic snoring.

Standing on the landing outside his room I noticed that the picture was crooked. Mum's picture. She'd found it in the garage when we moved in here. It was a large print called *The Three Marys* and it showed three women standing in long robes looking a bit mystical and swoony – like they were all in love or something. They were all gazing up into the sky and clutching their hands to their chests. The print was faded and had a green tinge to it. It was rippled in the middle because it hadn't been framed properly.

I hated that picture. It seemed stupid to have it up on the landing wall, romantic Bible bollocks in the middle of our crappy lives. But it was Mum's and she had liked it so I left it up. I stretched my hand out to straighten *The Three Marys* and as I reached up and touched the frame the first Mary looked at me. I swear to God she did. She'd been looking sadly up to heaven and when I touched the frame her head moved and her eyes met mine.

It must have been a split second – a tiny moment – but when she looked at me I noticed her eyes were the colour black, like mine, and it was like everything except our eyes looking at each other disappeared. I missed a breath and pulled my hand away and the print swung back into its crooked position and the Mary was looking at heaven again and I snapped back to where I'd been – the landing, the blue line of the pregnancy test, the note in my hand.

I'd already known really. I'd started to *feel* it. My belly had this slight curve to it that it never had before and I knew that soon I'd be able to see it really clearly. Everyone would. But until I saw the result it was like I could keep it inside me – like a secret story, just for me. And now there was a pregnancy test telling the story too: yes, you are going to have a baby, yes, you are going to be a mother, yes, yes, yes, this is real and there will be another person, there *is* another person under your skin. Maybe it was normal to see mad things when you felt mad. I straightened the picture, crept downstairs, put the note on the kitchen table and left the house, out, into the wet morning light.

2

Stephen

Oh. My. God. Batty McFelan and his daily friggin' OBSES-SION with school uniform. I swear, if there was only one kid in the school, Batty would tell him his tie was too short. Today it was my shoes. So what if Converse aren't 'school regulation'? (They're black with sliver trim – I got them ordered from New York and I'm telling you, they are bloody class.) I'd been wearing them since the start of term. And I know he noticed before today. Everyone noticed before today. Hello? That's the whole point! God. He was jealous, probably. Sitting there in his dog-shit coloured suit taking the register like he was bored out of his head. At least he gets paid to be bored. At least he didn't have to go to double Maths first lesson.

'Wear them tomorrow and it's detention,' he said. 'And don't roll your eyes at me, lad. I'm watching you today!'

I turned towards Mark for some moral support and, FFS,

Mark totally turned away and started chatting to Kyle Freeman! All right, I wasn't meant to acknowledge him in public but a sympathetic look might have been nice. Urgh. That was my morning. Not even 9 a.m. and it was already a completely rubbish day. And Nollaig wasn't even in. Who was I gonna bitch about McFelan to? I hoped she was just late. We'd be able to send notes during Maths at least.

But she never showed up. I texted her a few times. No reply. It wasn't particularly unusual for her to be absent. Some days she just didn't bother coming in, especially if she'd had a heavy time with her auld man the night before. He used to be OK, Nollaig's da. He was always a bit stern and stiff, the type that doesn't give much away, but most men round here are like that – you can't tell what's going on with them. It was different in my last school. People – I mean men, and boys – were a bit, well, softer round the edges. Anyway, in the last couple of years Nollaig's da had got worse. It was hard to remember the times when he wasn't always drunk, and sometimes he'd give her a slap. She didn't like me talking about it really. Things were bad for Nollaig. The days when she came to school and her eyes were red and she said hello with her teeth gritted – those were the days I knew not to ask. I know that sounds bad – like if you're someone's friend you should ask, but trust me I'd learnt when to ask and when to shut up, and so had everyone else, even the teachers.

In Maths we were doing quadratic equations and you could tell that nobody could be arsed. Craig and Arnie were giggling at the back of the class like a couple of primary school kids and every so often they'd look over at Emma McConkey and burst out laughing, but you knew they were doing it deliberately.

Emma was ignoring them, facing the board, looking as if she was concentrating really hard on the equation that Mrs Poole was drawing in big characters with a green pen. Rumour had it that Emma had been down the reccy with Arnie last week but she'd refused to give him what he was after. She'd pay for that.

'Oh, Craig and Arnie, put a sock in it!' said Mrs Poole, finally snapping.

'Put a cock in *what*, Miss?'

'That's it, Arnie! OUT!' She indicated to the door.

Arnie fist-bumped Craig as he swaggered out. I glanced over at Mark but he was pretending to be engrossed in the equations too. Arsehole. Why did I put up with him? But I knew why. When we were together, alone, when he wasn't pretending I didn't exist, he made me forget the way he treated me in school. I used to try and write it down so that I'd remember: 'Today Mark was a total prick in PE. He actually sniggered when Craig called me Queen of the Flower Fairies, as if he's not one himself! Twat!' But no matter how I tried to remember, I always forgot as soon as he paid me any attention. I hated myself for liking him.

'Stephen Corr. Snap out of it and start getting some work done, please!' Her voice was tense. The McThick Twins had rattled her.

'Yes, Miss.' I picked up my pen.

'He's dreaming about bums and fit blokes, Miss!' called a voice at the back of the room.

'Right, Craig!' She slammed the board marker down on her desk and the whole class jumped. 'I've had enough of this today. You can leave too.'

'Wha? I didn't swear! I was only messin'!'

11

'Out. Now.'

''SAKE!'

Craig scraped his chair back as noisily as he could, stood up and slammed it under the table again. He picked up his bag and gave Mrs Poole the evil eye as he left. She held his gaze, giving him the evil eye back. It was brilliant. The best thing to happen in Maths in ages. I smiled over at Emma and she smiled back. I wished Nollaig was here to see this. It was about time for Craig to get put in his place. Arnie was the really nasty one – I reckoned there wasn't much hope for him – but Craig? He was just a follower – Arnie's shadow, a jumped up wee shite. His family were loaded and everyone knew he'd get away with anything he liked at school because of who his da was and how much publicity he gave the school. When Daddy's in charge of half the city you can do what you like, can't you? School fairs, Christmas concerts, the opening of the new sports hall, there was Craig in the paper, like he was a model citizen, beaming out of his smart designer gear, with his posh lad boy-band haircut and his fat da, Councillor William McRoberts, standing there like he was Jesus Christ himself.

'What are you smirking at, Stephen?'

I snapped out of my daydream.

'Nothing, Miss.'

But it wasn't nothing. I'd be smirking all day remembering the look of shock on Craig's face when Mrs Poole kicked him out. Sweet!

But I wasn't smiling for long.

3

Nollaig

Leaving the house was easy. The gate squeaked as I closed it and I didn't bother doing the latch. I felt a little thrill run down my back thinking that I'd never have to be back here again. People feel sorry for kids who run away but I bet no one runs away unless it's worse for them at home. I wondered how many kids had made it. How many had got away and lived happily ever after. You only hear about the ones who end up becoming crack-heads and prostitutes or … let's not think of that. That wasn't going to be me.

There was a child's plastic Winnie the Pooh football in the next-door garden. One day maybe I'd have a house, maybe I'd be buying my kid plastic junk from the Pound Shop. Maybe everything would be OK. It had to be. I turned right and made my way to the corner going over my plan.

Up until I missed my period four months ago everything

was the same as it always had been. Boring school (but at least Stephen was there), hanging around town until as late as I could, coming home and trying to avoid Dad, doing whatever I needed to do (sometimes nicking a couple of quid off him, sometimes going out again for some food at the Spar, sometimes even doing some homework, depending on what mood I was in). But then, boom, everything was different and I ended up pregnant. Yeah, I know it doesn't happen quite like that, believe me I know, but I didn't want to think about how it happened.

I know I should have done the pregnancy test straight away but it wasn't that easy. For one thing, I was busy. There's a lot to sort out when you've got a dad like mine. The day-to-day stuff like getting food and having clean clothes – those things are easy. It's fooling everyone else that's the hard part. People notice things. Too many missed homeworks; falling asleep in class; bills not getting paid on time; the odd bruise on your face. You have to have a supply of stories that never run out. Your brain's buzzing all the time thinking of what's around the corner, who will be the next one to spot that your dad isn't behaving like a dad's supposed to.

And then you have to think about yourself too – about what'll happen if you do the things that other kids do to get through it. Did I feel like taking the stuff that Lee Riddell was selling round the back of Tesco? Too right I did.

'Imagine – how great would it be to *know* when you're next going to feel good?' he said to me one time, grabbing my hand and pressing two of the little pills into my palm. 'Imagine having control over it. That's what this stuff does. Life's shit, but you take this and will feel amazing. Nothing will hurt, you'll want to be alive, you'll *feel fucking alive . . .*'

But I put them back into his hand and he shrugged and walked off, shaking his head like I was a total loser. You just have to look at the kids who follow Lee round to see how much 'control' they have. Their eyes are dead – they're like ghosts. But I'd still been tempted. I wanted to have that control so badly and the best I could do was to console myself every night, as Dad snorted and stumbled around the house, with the idea that at least things couldn't get worse.

And then they did get worse.

Imagine waiting for that private girl thing that's meant to happen every month . . . and it being a week late. And then two weeks. And then three. And you know why. Every time you go to use the loo you hope it will be there and it's not and you *know* why. And you also know that as soon as you stop waiting for it to come you're going to have to start thinking about what's in its place. Thinking about it makes you feel sick. Or maybe that's not the reason you're feeling sick. And the thought of it makes you feel sick again. And you don't know whether you're actually, really sick or . . . You do a Google search on 'periods stopped, feeling sick, not pregnant' just to see if maybe it could possibly be something else, something else, please something else.

But it's not something else.

Imagine that.

Well, I didn't want to imagine it. I kept on hoping that my period would come back and I would forget about it. And then one day, about a month ago we were in Geography and we were watching a documentary about Africa. These people in a village had learnt a way to irrigate their fields with water from a nearby river so that they didn't have to go and fetch it in jugs. But they'd gotten these dirty hose pipes that had been used at some chemical plant and now people were dying because although all the food was growing it had been ruined because of the chemicals. Sharon Greer was sitting beside me sniffling into the arm of her jumper.

'Oh for goodness' sake, Sharon, do you need to go out?'

Mrs Mitchell could be a right bitch sometimes.

'Sorry, Miss. It's sad, that's all.'

'Not as sad as your trainers,' someone muttered. A few people giggled, Sharon pretended to ignore it, the teacher shushed everyone and we all went back to watching the documentary. Except now I couldn't concentrate on it. I pushed my chair back as far as it would go and leant back to take a glance at Sharon's shoes. There was nothing wrong with them. They weren't brightly coloured or weird looking. They didn't even look cheap. What they were was 'not expensive enough', and you could tell that they weren't right by looking at them, because they didn't have a logo. Suddenly, I wanted to cry as well.

I raised my hand.

'Yes? What now?'

'I need to be excused, Miss. Please, Miss, can I go to the loo?'

She tutted.

'Is it really urgent? There's only ten minutes left of this film and it's for your coursework.'

I could feel the tears filling up in my eyes. I knew if I blinked they'd spill out. I could see a couple of people had noticed because they were nudging each other and looking over at me.

'Yes Miss, sorry, I really have to go.'

'Fine . . . Go on then!'

I got out as quickly as I could, ran down the corridor to the toilets and locked myself in a cubicle. I took off my jumper and buried my face in it and I cried, hard. There was something growing inside me, something that was going to eventually be a person and I couldn't ignore it and the internet couldn't fix it. And I was going to have to look after that person and one day they'd have to go to school and get laughed at because I was going to do such a crap job. I wouldn't be able to get them the right clothes or help them to fit in. Or maybe I'd feed them wrong and they would die like those babies in the film. Because I didn't know what I was doing, because this was not meant to happen. And suddenly there was another thought.

I bolted out of the cubicle and almost knocked over a couple of sixth formers who'd come in to do their make-up before home time. I ran straight past the Geography room, to the other end of the corridor. I slammed my hand against the fire door bar and burst out into the car park. The public library was just down the street and I needed to be there, fast.

The woman in the library looked at me over her glasses with a pinched mouth. It was only 3 p.m. and everyone knew Glen High doesn't get out until half past.

'Geography project,' I panted.

She couldn't have believed me. I was a mess. I had run half a mile in the wind with my face streaming tears and snot. She took out a box of hankies from under the desk. The box was cream coloured and had lace around it. She still looked stern but I took a hankie and wiped my face and re-tied my hair and she said, 'That's better,' and she half smiled.

'Card?'

I handed it over.

'Computer number three.'

'Thanks.'

There are two computers in the library that are in little booth-type things, so you can be a bit more private. The rest are out in the open. Anyone can look over your shoulder and see if you're Googling how to make a bomb or writing a love email. Today I had to take an out-in-the-open computer but it didn't matter, I didn't even care if anyone saw me, I'd just say it was research for another class or something. Religious Studies. An essay about abortion. The funny thing was we had done that essay last year but now I couldn't remember anything about it.

I went straight to Google and typed in 'abortion', 'how many weeks pregnant' and 'UK law'.

The search engine threw up the results and I looked at the first few – advertisements for abortion clinics – not what I was looking for. Then one from the NHS. I clicked on the link. I found out straight away that I couldn't have an abortion in Northern Ireland unless I was really ill. My heart started to race. What did kids here do then? But that wasn't the information I needed right now either.

The library was warm and the moisture from people's raincoats was rising in half invisible clouds from the backs of their chairs. The windows were steamed up so you couldn't tell if it was still raining, but it probably was. If we get five days of sun in a row in Belfast it's a 'heatwave'. I wished that I had a drink of water.

I scanned down the page looking for a number.

24.

I was four months gone, tops. It was going to be OK! And then something happened. Before I could even start worrying about how I was meant to afford to get to England and pay for an abortion and do all that without anyone finding out. Before I had even typed anything else into Google. Before I could even think about how I felt about all of this, I just started feeling it. I didn't want to be pregnant, believe me, I really, *really* would rather have had a rare disease that had stopped my periods and made me throw up every morning and afternoon for three months. But I didn't want an abortion either. I couldn't imagine myself with a baby. But other people did it, didn't they? Maybe it would be OK. Maybe it would be better than OK. I just knew that, either way, I wanted to find out. That was all. I was sure.

I clicked the log-off button and stood up. My legs wobbled beneath me. I had almost had a plan and now I didn't. I put my hand on the computer desk to steady myself.

'You all right, love?' said the man next to me.

'Em, yeah. It's just a bit warm in here.'

'Here, here, have a wee drink, you should have said,' and he handed me his bottle of water. I recognised him. He used to work in the Spar. He used to slip me and Ciara Doherty the odd Black Jack for free when we were kids and our mums' backs were turned. He looked old now.

'Mr McEvoy?'

'Aye love, that's right. How's your da?'

I took the bottle. It was warm and the thought of drinking from it made me feel queasy. How's my da? He's barely human, Mr McEvoy. He's never sober any more. He makes me cook him dinner and then he doesn't eat it. He calls me 'Noll, love' when he needs me to go down the offy's, and then when he's had his fill he calls me a bitch and ten times worse. But what do you want to know about all that, eh? What does anyone want to know?

'Em, Dad's OK.' I handed the bottle back. 'Thanks, but I think I just need some air. I have to go, Mr McEvoy, nice to see you.'

'OK love, tell him I was asking after him, will you?'

'Yeah. I will, yeah.'

I checked the screen to make sure I'd logged out properly and I hoped he hadn't seen what I'd been looking at. I made a quick exit and headed to the play park on my way home. It had stopped raining but the park was almost empty, just a couple of kids on the swings with plastic bags under their bums to keep them dry. A woman was standing behind them in between the two swings, pushing both of them with one hand each, alternately. One swinging forward when the other went back.

I sat there and watched them for as long as they swung, giggling and shouting for a harder push. Back, forth, quick and regular, like two clocks in time with themselves but not each other, tick, tock, tick, tock, or a complicated drum beat that somehow works although it sounds like it shouldn't. That was when I started to think up my plan, right there on the park bench, with my school trousers getting soaked through, watching those little laughing kids making sense out of that crazy rhythm. I knew I had to take a chance on something. If it wasn't going to be an abortion then I had to think, because things were about to change in a big way, and it wasn't going to involve bringing a kid up in my dad's house, no way.

4

Stephen

Breaktime. I was standing to the side of the lockers at the bottom of the stairs with my back to the wall. Nollaig had showed me this spot when I'd first started at Glen High. It was the best hiding place and the best vantage point in the whole school. You could see up the stairs to get a look at who was coming down before they could see you. If it was someone you wanted to avoid you could duck underneath the stairs quickly. The funny thing was that these days I spent most of the time looking for people, well, one person that I wanted to see, rather than people I wanted to avoid. But normally he didn't want to see me. Heh. Maybe I should have given up my spot to him and then he would have been better at hiding from me. Maybe someday, when I wasn't so obsessed with him, I would.

Anyway, the other good thing about that spot was that you were practically hidden from the people walking past in the adjoining corridor as well. It meant you could spend the whole of break or lunchtime there when you were meant to be in the cafeteria. Noll and I had scoped it from all angles when I first arrived at the school. The space was just about big enough to hide us both a couple of years ago. These days we had to be a bit more careful. Nollaig. I missed her today. I was just reaching into my pocket for my phone when I heard the voice.

'You should not be here at breaktimes. You know the rules.'

God's sake. It was McFelan again. Of all people. But how did he see me? I looked down at the floor. The strap of my bag was sticking out beyond the locker. He must have seen it. I couldn't believe I'd been so stupid. I knew what was coming next.

'Office, lad. Now.'

He really had it in for me today. There was no point in arguing. I followed him to the principal's office.

I liked Mr Jakks's office. I know that's a strange thing to say, but I liked sitting in there. It was comfortable and bright and, unlike the rest of the school rooms, which were bland and overgrowing with piles of worn out textbooks, the principal's office felt organised. Mr Jakks's room had warm, sand coloured walls and a thick terracotta carpet. He sat on a soft black leather chair in front of his huge desk. I sat opposite him, beside Batty McFelan, feeling tiny. It was warmer in his office than in the rest of the school and I wondered if we could make the chat last beyond the end of breaktime and into triple Science. That'd be sweet.

I wasn't worried about being in trouble. I'd been here before because of uniform regulations. There was the time I dyed my hair blue and then the time I refused to remove my coloured wristbands. I knew that Jakks wasn't too concerned about kids' uniforms as long as they behaved themselves generally. If you complied once you'd been told off then you knew it would be OK for another while. So I let my hair go back to its natural colour, and I took off my wristbands. And I'd wear the proper shoes tomorrow. I'd be annoyed to have to hide my lovely new Cons but it wasn't worth a load of hassle and if I behaved myself now I could probably get away with wearing them later on. Once or twice anyway, I reckoned.

I relaxed into the blue cushion of my seat as Mr Jakks chatted calmly on the phone to some parent about their child's late homeworks. Batty's face was purple with the anticipation. You'd think he'd seen me nickin' money out of the school canteen or something. He looked as if he was going to have a heart attack if Mr Jakks didn't finish his phone call soon.

As Jakks hung up the phone Batty sighed deeply, which made Mr Jakks raise an eyebrow.

'Mr McFelan. Stephen.' He addressed us in a slow, deep voice. 'How can I help you?'

'Well!'

And McFelan was away, ninety miles per hour, relating the story about my 'inappropriate footwear' and 'general attitude' and 'following the rules about breaktime' and 'setting a poor example to the younger ones' and blah-de-bloody-blah.

I just sat there, staring at him. I imagined my eyes boring a hole into his skull. What would I see in there? Not much. A tiny, hard brain, like a small lump of coal, huffing and puffing and grinding its gears to enable him to make the odd grunt.

'It's no laughing matter!' he barked at me.

Oops! Smirking again. This time I stopped and made myself

look serious. I hated Batty but I didn't mind auld Jakks and I didn't want him to think I really did have a bad attitude.

Jakks was quiet. He had his forefingers pressed against one another, touching his lips. He waited until Batty had finished his crazy rant and then he said something and suddenly I didn't feel quite so confident any more.

'Mr McFelan. Thank you for bringing these issues to my attention. If you wouldn't mind, I would like to speak to Stephen on his own for a few minutes.'

McFelan didn't like that. You could tell he'd been waiting for the kill. He was almost drooling, the auld fascist. But I didn't like it either. Speak to me alone? Why? That made everything sound serious. Suddenly I wanted McFelan to stay.

'I don't mind if he stays,' I said.

'Thank you, Stephen, but I'd like a word in private.'

Batty's mouth was a straight line but I couldn't even relish his annoyance. He muttered a 'thank you' to Jakks and backed out of the room, shutting the door quietly.

Once he was gone the room seemed colder. I knew it couldn't have just been about uniform, but I heard myself apologising about the shoes as if I'd committed the crime of the century.

He frowned.

'It's not your shoes, Stephen. Well, not just your shoes.'

'Then, what, Sir?'

'Well ...' he spoke carefully, making sure he got the words right, 'there was an incident this morning. In Maths.'

'Maths?'

'With two other boys.'

Arnie and Craig? But what had that got to do with me? Had

Mrs Poole been complaining about me smirking? That was bound to be it. She was in such a bad mood. She was overreacting, but I was glad that's all it was.

'I'm sorry for smirking, Sir.'

'Excuse me?'

'Smirking. You know, smiling. In Mrs Poole's lesson. I don't realise I'm doing it, Sir. I know it's rude, but—'

'I don't know what you mean, Stephen. This isn't about smirking.'

He looked at me gravely and ran a hand through his hair.

'Stephen, I'm not excusing what Craig said. Not at all. I don't tolerate bad language in school.'

I remembered Craig's comments about me dreaming of bums and fit lads. But Arnie had said 'cock' to a teacher, surely that was worse? And anyway, what did this all have to do with me? Was he afraid I was gonna get my mum to complain or something? As if!

'It's OK, Sir. It doesn't really bother me. Not any more, anyway.'

He rubbed his eyes and sighed as if I wasn't getting it. He was right. I had no idea what was going on.

'I know you're an individual, Stephen. It's good, in a way, to be an individual. You know, to, em, express yourself and what-not. I just ... look, I know things haven't been easy for you at home and I um, er ...'

Whatever he was getting at it still wasn't clear. Something to do with my shoes, and Craig being a dick, and now my mum and what happened before we came here? But the trouble with Rob was ages ago. Nope, I was definitely stumped.

And then he said something else and it began to click into place.

'Stephen, in life, sometimes, if you want to avoid trouble, you have to, em, make the effort to fit in.'

'What?'

Suddenly I forgot about being in trouble, about not wanting Jakks to think I had a bad attitude. I could see what he meant now. He'd chosen them, over me. Bloody Arnie, and Craig and his rich da. I was getting the blame for them being idiots. OK, so I'd worn the wrong shoes to school. But he was actually choosing those knuckle-dragging twats over me. How could he? I hadn't even said a word in Maths.

He must have read my mind because his face went red and he couldn't meet my eyes. But it didn't stop him.

'I want you to know that you're not in any trouble, Stephen, but . . .'

'Why would I be in trouble, Sir?'

He ignored me.

'I've sent Craig's father a letter and, like I said, we don't tolerate bad language in this school, but . . .'

'But what?'

My tone was sharp and that's when he met my eyes.

'You have to toe the line, Stephen. I've heard . . . I've heard that sometimes you act, well, different. On purpose. Do you know what I mean?'

I did. But he could go to hell.

'No, Sir. What do you mean?'

'Just that . . . well, the other boys sometimes find it hard to know how they should act around you, and that maybe you could make it a bit easier on yourself sometimes.'

'Easier on *them*, you mean?'

'No, no. On you. I'm thinking about you.'

Sometimes when I get angry I get this picture in my head. Rob. I picture him standing in an alley holding his big, black leather Bible, and I'm beating the crap out of him. It helps me cope, that picture. Instead of saying what I want to say, or doing what I want to do, instead of running out of Jakks's office and telling him where he could stick his fake concern, I stuck the boot into Rob in my head. Over, and over. And when he was lying there, bleeding, and my brand new Cons were covered in his blood, I looked at Mr Jakks, full in the face, and said,

'Thanks for your concern, Sir. I'll try and be less gay in future. Can I go now?'

He sighed.

'Yes, Stephen. I really am just thinking of you, you know.'

I turned away from him in silence and shut the door behind me.

5

Nollaig

Belfast is full of churches. Some of them are enormous and you can tell loads of people go there because on Sunday morning there are cars everywhere and then it's quiet for the rest of the day. But St Anthony's is small and it's never busy. You hardly ever see anyone around going in or coming out and that's one of the reasons I picked it. When we were kids everyone used to say it was haunted and that if you went there at midnight on a full moon you could see the shadow of a banshee at the window, and then you'd die within twenty-four hours. We used to dare each other to run past it when it was dark. I don't know when we stopped being afraid of it. Everyone just ignores it now.

I don't go to church. We can add that to our list of 'Great Things About Having an Alcoholic Da'. We never once had an argument about going to church. I don't believe in God and I don't think he believes in anything.

Getting to the corner was the easy part but then I had to walk past Stephen's house. St Anthony's was a few streets away. Not far, but I wasn't sure I could make it to the end of even this row of houses. Stephen's was number twelve.

Stephen is the best thing in my life. He is probably the main reason I didn't run off before, or worse. We've known each other since we were thirteen – his first day at our school. I found him getting hassled by Glen High's number one resident arseholes. I remembered their big gurning faces close to his, giving him all kinds of shit. But they were the last people I wanted to be thinking about today of all days, so I tried to focus on Stephen.

He still looks the same now as he did then too – a mess of light brown hair, these days made darker with whatever hair product he uses to make the mess look like mess-on-purpose. And brown eyes. His skin's better now but he has the same smile – wide and a bit like a cat's – he can smile with just the edges of his mouth. His nose turns up at the end, just slightly, so he looks like he's posh but he isn't, and he's just as generous and kind as he was then. Not that we haven't ever fallen out, but I know he's on my side and I'm on his, and that's how it is with us – we've got each other's backs. He rescues me and I rescue him and we get through stuff.

Standing at the top of the street I wondered what on earth I was doing, preparing to walk past and chuck all of that away. But I couldn't knock on his door. After everything he'd done for me, it would have been unfair to involve him. I knew what he'd say as well: 'C'mon, Noll, you have to tell someone. You have to let someone help you this time. Please. Tell someone.' He might have convinced me, and I just couldn't risk that. It would mean me being taken into care – a home, like the one Lee Riddell used to be in. It was so bad he used to run away from it all the time, and he's not the type of fella that runs away from fights, if you know what I mean. He said it was full of kids who beat each other up over drugs, and any of the girls that got pregnant had their kids taken off them. Well, that wasn't happening to me, no way.

I dug out my mum's ancient CD player. The 'play' button made a 'chunk' noise and I put the headphones on. They're from the '80s and they're these big cans that cover your whole ears. They look like something you'd imagine a fat old wedding disco DJ would wear, standing with his belly bopping to the tunes on his scratchy record player, bottle of beer in his hand. Normally I would never put them on in public but this morning I didn't care because I needed something to get me down the street, past Stephen's house.

The CD started skipping almost immediately. I had to stop it and take it out and blow on it and put it back in again. My hands were getting sweaty now, I just needed to get going. 'Chunk.' This time the music was fine. The shadows of the clouds in the puddles turned silvery and the rain had stopped and I let myself hear the words and then I started walking, concentrating on the rhythm rather than the houses. It was Bob Marley. Not the kind of music I normally like but I play it when I want to remember her. She used to sing it in the car. He was singing about not worrying, how everything's going to be all right. I used to listen to that and think 'Well, how does he know?'

I walked past Stephen's house without looking. I kept my eyes straight ahead and by the time I got to the end of the street the song was finishing and there were tears running down my face and I think I was singing the words to myself in a whisper over and over and if anyone had seen me then they would have known something was going on, but no one did and I took that as a good sign. I wiped my face with the sleeve of my hoody and looked ahead. I could see the spire of St Anthony's now.

St Anthony's was going to be a stop gap. Somewhere to stay for maybe five days, a week tops. A couple of years ago this kid from our school went missing. She'd been getting picked on for being fat and it was doubly crap for her because her parents were splitting up, and not in a nice way. Maybe there's never a nice way to split up, but you know what I mean. They'd show up at the school and scream at each other about whose turn it was to take her home, in front of everyone, which just gave the bullies more to go on. Idiots.

So everyone knew all her business about why her parents were getting a divorce (her mum yelled it across the playground, that it was 'that wee slut from Finaghy' her dad had been seeing) and I guess one day she'd just had enough, of everyone. She never showed up for school and she never showed up at home.

Five days. That's how long people talked about it. That's how long it was on the news. Pathetic or what? You had people crying in class and everything, people claiming to be her 'best friend' when really everyone knew she had no friends. Her mum and dad went on the telly pretending to be these great, loving parents, and saying how they couldn't understand why their kid had run off. And after five days something else happened and the world moved on and she was forgotten, like all the other kids that run off.

The news moved on to the latest boy band to split up. The kids in school found someone else to pick on. Even her parents moved on – her dad moved in with the girl from Finaghy and her mum got married to one of the journalists who'd covered the story and last year they had a kid together. The girl never came back and no one had waited for her anyway. Life goes on. Crap, isn't it? But not for me. The sooner everyone forgot about me, the better.

So the plan was that I'd stay at St Anthony's, hide out there in the empty church and lie low until people had stopped looking (and let's face it, there weren't going to be many people looking. Dad would probably forget about ten minutes after he'd read the note.) and then I could move on. It wasn't going to be for long. If I could find somewhere to stay for just four months then I'd turn sixteen and I couldn't be taken into care. I'd be heavily pregnant by then so maybe I'd be able to get a house and some benefits, at least until I found a job. I was sure I could manage for that long. Sixteen weeks, maybe in Dublin or somewhere busy where people don't have time to wonder who you are or where you came from. Maybe if the church thing worked out I could stay for a couple of weeks at a time in different churches – that's only a few moves. I'd figure it out anyway. Everything was gonna be all right.

I stuffed the massive headphones and CD player into my bag and turned the corner, street number two. This was going to be a doddle. Ten minutes max and I'd be at the church, ready to start my new life. It felt good to be doing something – making a journey, getting away.

That was when people's doors started opening and they started coming out of their houses. Kids in school uniform, mums in their pyjamas with coats on. Some of them got into cars but most of them closed their doors and started walking down the street, walking towards me. Shit. Loads of them would see me. I couldn't let that happen.

To my left there was a narrow entry. I knew it – we used to cut across it to get to the playing fields when we were kids and then someone was stabbed there and everyone stopped using it. A thin walkway with parallel fences hiding the backs of houses on either side. It was dark and I could see there were bins blocking the other end but I had no choice. It would make the walk to the church longer but it was probably going to be safer than heading straight into a load of kids and their mums.

Cursing my stupidity (who plans a runaway attempt when the entire world is on their way to work or school or the dole office?) I turned down the entry. The gravel crunched under my feet and got stung by the wet nettles growing in huge green masses, almost as tall as me, the whole way down the path. I stuck my hands up inside my coat sleeves and covered my face as best I could with the hood of my top. Something moved behind the bins at the end of the alley. Probably just a dog. I could hear a woman shouting at her kids to get out of bed cos they'd missed the bus already. She was yelling and cursing at them but there was no response. I hurried past. There was no roof over the entry but it felt like there was. The sky seemed dark and low and I was walking as fast as I could but it felt like there was further to go with every step.

I looked over my shoulder and the start of the path seemed far away as well. I couldn't remember it being this long when I was a kid. The woman stopped shouting and then there was silence. Complete silence. No car doors slamming in the distance, no hum of traffic, no dogs barking. Not even the shuffle of crisp bags getting blown about by the wind. Nothing. It was weird and for the first time since I left the house, for the first time in a really long time, I felt scared to be on my own. I started running and now I could feel myself getting closer to the end and the thing behind the bins moved again but I kept running.

I've never been a claustrophobic kind of person. Stephen and I went camping one time. We found this tent in his roof space and his mum said it was hers – she'd bought it when he was born, thinking they could go off camping together for holidays, but she'd only tried it once. There was a storm in the middle of the night and the tent started to collapse on top of them. Stephen was crying and she'd had to get up in just her pants and t-shirt in the howling wind and rain and bundle him into the car and take down the tent before it blew away. That was the end of their camping trip.

She laughed until she was crying when she told us that story. The storm had woken up everyone on the campsite and all these middle aged dads had emerged from their tents to nip over to the toilet block, bleary eyed and also in their pants, and a few of them had come over to ask her if she needed any help and one of them turned out to be a teacher that she'd had at school. So there she was, in her pants and a t-shirt, with a tent that was becoming the world's largest kite and lifting her off her feet and a crying baby in a buggy and her Geography teacher in his pants and all of them getting soaked and yelling polite small talk over the lashing rain and gales:

'OH IT'S YOU! HOW ARE YOU, JUDITH?'

'OH MY GOODNESS! I'M FINE. WORKING AT ASDA NOW, SIR.'

'OH, YOU CAN CALL ME MARCUS. I'M NOT YOUR TEACHER ANY MORE!'

'EM, OK MARCUS. BAD WEATHER, EH?'

'YES, VERY POOR . . .'

So anyway, we found the tent and thought we'd go on a trip of our own, but Stephen lasted precisely two hours before he started freaking out and saying he couldn't breathe and he needed to have the tent door unzipped. But neither of us could stand it because of (guess what?) the rain coming in and so we packed up and went home. I was in a mood with Stephen the whole way home. But now, running down the silent, dark entry and feeling the sky closing in, I started to understand how he'd felt. My heart was pounding and I couldn't get to the end of a breath but it wasn't because of running. I wished I could unzip the silence and I started longing for the mad woman to start screaming at her kids again.

Closer to the bins now and I started to relax a little. The thing near to the bins wasn't a dog, it was a person, probably some fella waiting for his mate. I stopped running and told myself to wise up. You have to do that sometimes. If you expect bad things sometimes you will imagine them happening and then sometimes the imagining will turn into something real and it will be all your own fault. Stephen says it's called Self-Fulfilling Prophecy and that you have to make sure you catch yourself on if you start thinking about too many scary or bad things. I think he's right. If you think you'll fail an exam and you don't do any work because you think there's no point since you'll fail, then you *will* fail and you'll never know whether it was true destiny or just a Self-Fulfilling Prophecy (which is basically just acting like an idiot). Stop. Breathe. Five breaths. Focus on where I'm going to end up. The church. Safety. I could do this. The end of the alley had to be, what? Fifteen steps away, tops. Start counting them out: One. Two. Three. Four. Five. Six. Seven . . .

The boy who was waiting for his mate saw me. He looked right at me. I expected him to turn away but he didn't. He fumbled in his pocket for something. The bins shook a little as he passed them, walking to where I was standing, now frozen. I could see him more clearly now. An older guy – maybe nineteen or so, or older. He was wearing a black coat and the hood of it covered almost his whole face so I could only see his mouth clearly and he was holding something that was a dull steel colour and he held it out towards me. A knife. The mouth spoke.

'Give it to me.'

Give what? How many things did I have to give? I knew I had to answer but I was afraid to speak because maybe it would be a Self-Fulfilling Prophecy and if I asked him what he wanted I'd have to give it to him.

'Give. It. To. Me.'

His voice was very quiet, like a whisper, but I could hear him clearly and I wondered if there was anyone else around who could hear him too. He looked over his shoulder as if he'd been thinking the same. What if I shouted, would anyone hear me? But I had come here to avoid being seen. Was it all going to be over so soon? I thought about Dad and about him starting to wake up now, how he'd have a thumping headache and how he'd be cursing himself for being awake when he'd rather sleep forever. You've never seen a bad mood like my dad with a hangover. I wasn't going back to that.

'What do you want?'

Whatever it was, he could have it. He motioned with his hand.

'Give.'

He was moving now. Still holding out the knife. It was a small knife. It had a black handle and it looked cheap, like the kind of kitchen knife you'd find in the Pound Shop that'd last for a month and then break when you were chopping spuds and cut your hand. It could still hurt someone, though.

He was coming towards me with his head bowed so I couldn't see his face. He was so tall that I could have tried to look up under the hood but I didn't dare. It was bad enough that he had seen me. If I saw him too he'd have even more of a reason to make sure I wouldn't be able to report him. So I kept my eyes lowered too as I threw my bag towards him.

'Is this it? Is this what you want?' I could hardly hear myself but I couldn't make my voice any louder. 'You can have it, just let me go, OK? Just leave me alone, OK?'

He lowered the knife and stooped to pick up the bag. I wasn't going to hang around for a chat. I legged it, scrambling past the bins. I ran around the corner in the vague direction of the church and I didn't stop until the stitch in my side hurt so much that I started worrying that maybe it wasn't a stitch, maybe something was wrong with the baby. I stopped and stood behind an old phone box that smelled of piss. I clutched my side and

37

bent over and retched, gulping down the freezing air. Behind me the streets were buzzing quietly with a morning already begun. Through open windows I could hear washing machines and Jeremy Kyle on the telly and the street was empty and the tall guy with the knife was nowhere and now I had nothing. The money was gone, and the food. Oh God, what now? Maybe this was it. A sign. A message from the universe that I was just being stupid. Maybe all I deserved was that care home with the crack-heads and fights. But what about the baby? What did it deserve? Jesus, he could have killed it with that stupid knife. He wouldn't even have known. If he'd stuck it into me, he could've killed it. It. Him. Or her. Us. I crouched down against the dirty glass of the phone box.

My brain thumped against my skull and I wondered whether to cry or not. I could, I thought. I could sit down right here on the pavement and cry out loud until someone came over to help. A kind person, someone rich who would take pity on me and agree to give me a load of cash until I was sorted with a job. Yeah right.

I sat, hunched down by that phone box, for about fifteen minutes, trying to stop shaking by making up my little fantasy about the kind rich person and watching people who were luckier than me go past. I couldn't go to pieces. I couldn't. Something else would have to happen instead . . .

A man with a briefcase who was wearing a dark suit and looking important. A fat woman holding the hands of two small kids in school uniform who were clutching brightly col-oured lunch bags. I saw a girl about my age pushing a buggy. She was dressed in a tracksuit and the bottoms of the legs of it were too long. There were zips at the bottom and they were undone up to her ankles and you could see her trainers poking out of the flappy material. Bit worn but good ones, Nike. She was talking to someone on a pink flip-up phone as she pushed the buggy. The kid must have been about two years old and he was waggling bare legs and eating a packet of crisps. When the girl saw me looking at her she held the phone away from her ear.

'Seen enough?'

She looked me up and down and sneered like I was something she'd just scraped off her Nikes. And then she went back to her chat and she tossed her hair and walked off with the waggly kid who tossed the crisp bag onto the pavement as they left.

I probably should have gone home. Spoken to someone, a teacher or something. Maybe they could have helped and maybe that care home would have been OK, and maybe they wouldn't have taken my baby off me ... or maybe if they did there would be a way to get it back ... But no. I looked at that girl. She hadn't known how it would all turn out either. I bet she went through all the maybes too. And then she made decisions and it turned out how it turned out. Simple, in a way. One day when it was my kid kicking their legs out of a buggy and yelling for more crisps then I'd be able to think to myself, I did what I could. I did *everything* I could, and I made some decisions and some of them were rubbish but I really did try my best. And the best thing now was to find the church and see if I could find a way to carry on with the plan and if I couldn't do that I'd have to go back and talk to a teacher and hope for the best and keep out of Dad's way. Even if that guy had taken everything. I put my hand on my stomach and watched as it finally stopped trembling. No. He hadn't taken everything.

I looked over the top of the phone box and I could see the church's spire a couple of streets away. There were grey clouds hovering over it and I stuck my hands in my empty pockets and started walking.

6

Stephen

It was stupid really, skipping Art, because it was my best subject. It was the best thing about school really, Art, and Nollaig of course. I'd been working on a project for my exam coursework and it's what I wanted to do after school – to go to Art college, be a proper artist.

But today I needed a break. I locked the cubicle door and sat on the toilet lid, drawing my legs up so that no one would be able to look under and see me here. Old Crispy wouldn't check the register to see if I should be in class. I never skipped Art and he'd just assume I was sick. Arnie and Craig weren't in Art so there'd be nobody there to tout on me. Kyle Freeman was mates with them sometimes but I didn't think he'd say anything. I just needed some space.

I took out my phone. No messages.

'Where the fk are you?' I typed. 'Are you ill? Am havin shit day ☹'

I clicked 'send' and the phone beeped loudly.

'Who's in there?'

I jumped. Crap. I sat as still as I could, balancing on the wobbly black plastic.

'C'mon. Who is it? Whoever it is, you should be in class.'

It was Marty, the caretaker. I put my feet on the floor. I wanted to be in Art class really anyway.

'Only me.' I half smiled as I swung open the cubicle door.

'Stephen?' He looked up. 'What are you up to?' He was wiping the taps with an old blue cloth.

'Felt sick. I'm OK now, though.'

He raised an eyebrow.

'Sick of school, eh?'

He was a good guy, Marty. He never touted on kids unless they were up to serious badness, and he'd let you check lost property for old PE gear if you'd forgotten your kit.

'Yeah, actually.' I grinned at him and he smiled back and continued wiping the taps.

'Well, don't you go ruining your chances, will you? Life's not any easier on the other side of the school gates.'

Somehow I doubted that. I didn't mind school but I hated Arnie and Craig. I knew there'd always be people like them but at least in the real world you wouldn't be stuck in a room with them most of the day.

'Oh cheer up,' Marty continued, squeezing the cloth out and spraying the next set of taps. 'Least you're not cleaning the bogs, eh? Away, off to class!'

He waved me off with a wink and I turned towards the door. My phone buzzed in my pocket. Noll! But it wasn't Noll. It was Mark. He never texted me during the week. I read the message.

NEED TO TALK. MEET ME AFTER SCHOOL IN PARK.

My heart thumped. I knew what it meant. I'd been waiting for a message like this for a while now. On the way back to class I let myself imagine the meeting the way I wanted it to go. I'd enter the park by the rusty green side gates and Mark would be there on the bench next to the rose garden. He'd be wearing his old beaten up black leather jacket over his school blazer and his dark fringe would be flopping over half of his face. He'd notice me, look up and smile.

'Hey,' he'd say, and I'd sit down beside him, casually.

'Hiya. I got your message. What's up?' I'd reply.

'Nothing. I mean, nothing to worry about anyway. I hope I didn't freak you out.'

I'd smile and shake my head and he'd reach for my hand, and as he did the rose bushes would grow in front of our eyes. They'd grow taller and taller, building a canopy around us, all different shades of pink and red, and soon we'd be completely hidden together and we could say what we wanted, do whatever we wanted. We'd join our other hands together and I'd look up at his face and reach up to push his fringe to the side and . . .

'Where've you been, Stephen?' Crispy didn't even look up from his marking. 'Hmmm? Come in and sit down, please.'

I found my spot and glanced at the clock. 3 p.m. The stinking day was almost over. Good riddance. I opened my file and took out my project – a study of the flowers in the park – roses, close up – the way their petals felt softer than silk. I'd wanted to capture how impossible it was that the same plant could tear your skin and make you bleed with its sharp thorns. I'd spent weeks sketching, working in watercolours, trying out acrylics, even making a collage with different fabrics. Now I just felt like scrapping the whole thing. I stared at the pages in front of me. Maybe I should draw sports cars like the other lads. That's what they all wanted, wasn't it? Jakks, Rob, most blokes really. Play the game, Stephen, don't be such a poof, flowers are for girls and gays, stop noticing colours, start being a dickhead . . .

The bell went and I looked at my page. I'd sketched in dark shadows on all the flowers. It was ruined.

7

Nollaig

I didn't go into the church through the front door, obviously. I'd been counting on there being a way to break in round the back. I crept round the side, looking behind me every five seconds. Every noise – a bird shuffling in the hedge, a car passing – made my chest thump a bit harder. Come on, I told myself, pull yourself together, Noll. The back of the church was overgrown and the weeds were tangled and high over the graves – a good place for hiding. I felt my hands starting to shake again, but no, I wouldn't let that bastard get to me. Think of what was ahead: safety. The future. I thought of Ciara Doherty.

Ciara and I used to mess about here when we were kids. It was a brilliant place to play because no one came here and there was a small graveyard out the back – old and wild with weeds and brambles We had this game where you had to chase each other round the graves and you could hop over them but if you put one foot on someone's grave, or if you got caught, it meant you were dead and if you were dead you had to lie down on the grave with your arms folded over your chest for one minute. Then when you got up you had to turn to the gravestone and if you could read the name on it you had to apologise to the dead person whose grave you'd been lying on: 'Forgive me, George McGraw, for lying on your grave.'

I only ever saw the inside of the church once. It was at my cousin's baby's baptism. My mum made me go with her. I was only about eight years old and I can't remember much about it except that it was really boring and the kid screamed the place down, which I thought was dead funny because my cousin and her family were such snobs. They were always going on about moving to Australia and how much money they were making these days and blah blah blah. My mum couldn't stand them either but she said we had to go because it was 'the right thing to do' and after all it wasn't the baby's fault. After my mum died they did go to Australia. I guess they were worried they'd get lumbered with me if they hung around. Good riddance anyway.

The other thing I remember about that baptism was that there was a big window at the back of the church. It had a huge angel bending over a woman who looked a bit worried and it was really colourful, lots of blues, reds and yellows. I kept craning my head around to look at it and my mum kept poking me in the side because she thought I was trying to annoy the kids in the seat behind us. To be honest I was quite excited about going to see that window again. This time I'd get a really good look.

The church looked smaller now than I remembered it. The

graveyard at the back was even more overgrown. Crooked head-stones stuck out of the ground at weird angles but you could hardly see most of the graves for nettles and thorns. Maybe Ciara and I were the last kids to play in it. I turned to the stone building to see if I could find a way in.

There was a wooden door, the green paint peeling off the flaky wood. A brass label screwed to the wall beside it read 'CRYPT'. The word made me think of Dracula and dead hands curling from the rising lids of dusty coffins. A stupid thought. It was probably just an empty cellar, right? My hands shook slightly as I felt for a lock but the door didn't have one. I gave it a shove to see what would happen and it just opened. It was easy. I don't know why I was surprised really because who'd want to break into an ancient old church anyway? What would they steal? Bibles? Haha.

That door led down a long flight of stairs. It was getting darker and I wished I'd brought a torch but I hadn't thought about it because it wasn't night time when I left. I put my hand on the cold plaster wall to feel my way down and parts of it crumbled beneath my fingers. Once I'd shut the door behind me the only thing I could see was a thin line of yellow light tracing the outline of it. I tried to think about the Bible thieves again but it wasn't that funny any more.

At the bottom of the stairs there was another door which led into an even darker space. I felt along the wall for a light switch. I had to close the door behind me so that when I turned on the light none would escape. There wouldn't be anyone around to see a light going on but I couldn't take a chance on it. The fullness of the dark felt like someone putting their hands over my eyes. I clicked the switch and nothing happened for a second, then the tube lights on the ceiling started to flicker. I squinted as they finally pinged into brightness. It was a room for children.

It had been painted in primary colours and there was a huge, badly drawn mural of Noah's ark on one of the walls. The elephants were smaller than the ostriches and Noah only had four fingers. There was a small bookshelf with a load of Bible stories and a biscuit tin full of fat crayons and felt tips with no lids. But it was the little chairs and tables that got me. Each tiny chair representing a little person. I wondered if they were happy or sad. I thought about Ciara and me chasing each other round the graves and yelling 'You're going to die! You're going to SO die!' and laughing until we were crying. But shut up about that. Enough. This was going to be my happy place. This would be where I stopped being a helpless kid. I saw another door.

I was in the room behind the kids' room. It must have been an old store cupboard or something. It had been hard to open the door. I'd had to push really hard and squeeze in through the tiny opening and when I did the door sprang back and shut and I was in darkness again. I tried the light. Nothing. I started to feel my way around. Something near the door felt hard, and then soft and then hard again. An armchair? Yes. I put my hand where the seat might be and it just felt like springs. But it was enough. I couldn't do any more. I was exhausted. I took off my hoody and tried to bunch it and shove it over the springs and then I curled up on it and I put my head on the wooden arm.

I didn't know whether my eyes were closed or not but they must have been because next thing I knew I was waking up and choking with a mouth full of dust and wondering where I was. When you wake up and it's pitch black like that you panic a bit wondering if you're really awake or in some kind of nightmare. It took a few seconds for me to remember where I was. My head hurt and my mouth felt like I'd been eating gravel. Ow. It was sore getting up. The springs had been jamming into my back and I wondered what time it was. How long had I been asleep? I forced the door back and mashed myself through the tiny gap again and into the kids' playroom.

There was a sink at the side of the room with a cupboard underneath it. I stumbled over and turned the tap and put my mouth to the running water, gulping it down. It was so cold that it hurt but I felt better instantly. It was like I'd been dead and now I was coming back to life. I splashed some of the water on my face. The cupboard had a kettle and these dainty china teacups and saucers with little purple flowers on them. There were two plain biscuits left in the tin and my stomach growled as I wolfed them down. I'd forgotten that I was hungry but now I felt it. A gnarly ache. A wave of nausea rose in my chest and I retched but managed to keep the biscuits down. But it wasn't enough. I was starving. I'd been hungry before but it was different now. A low growl that just kept going and going. I started wondering if the baby would hear it and get frightened and that made it worse.

Sitting on the floor of the kids' room I finally started to cry. Maybe this was it. Maybe this was the end of 'everything I could do' and I had to just give up now and go back home and face Dad and forget about my dream of changing everything. That's when the lights went out. At first I froze thinking that someone was in the church and had somehow switched them off. Well, it truly was the end then. I cried hard. It wasn't fair. It was over. And then I heard it.

'sssssshhhhhh'

A silence. It happened again.

'sssssshhhhhh'

And that was all. I had stopped crying to listen to whatever it was. Maybe just the trees outside? But would they be so clear? It was more like a voice, like someone comforting a child. But then it was gone. And the quiet that it left filled the entire room. It had been quiet before, of course, but something had changed – it wasn't just that there was no noise – it was like the room was full of peace.

The lights flickered back on and the big silence disappeared and I was back, sitting on the floor in a kids' Sunday School room, wondering what had just happened. The calm that was left in the room felt like something had swept through and just turned everything back to normal. It was all so ordinary. And I felt ordinary too, like here was this problem: I was hungry and had no food, and now I had to do something about that. It was so strange, like someone had swept away the pressure of all my bad thoughts, all the unfairness, and left just the problem to be solved. And maybe I could solve it. I could have a go at least. Maybe this kind of thing happened when you were pregnant. Maybe having a baby inside you made you focus on what needed to be done.

It couldn't make the lights go out, though, could it?

It was probably an electrical fault. A coincidence. I'd think about it later because right now I needed to get food.

50

Stephen and I saw this thing on telly once. It was one of those reality shows where they get people to swap lives for a bit and they always end up having big fights with the people they have to get along with. Anyway in this episode this woman had to go and live with a family who lived in a caravan and they didn't have jobs and their kids didn't have to go to school. If they wanted food they got it from the bins at Tesco, which sounds disgusting, but they would get some amazing stuff. They'd sneak out in the middle of the night and raid the bins for all this food that'd been chucked out because it was the day before its sell-by date and no one would buy it – croissants and yoghurt and stuff, even fruit that hasn't gone bad and bread that hasn't gone mouldy.

'We should do that some time, Noll!' he said, sprawled out on our sofa, eating crisps.

Dad was in bed, asleep. Sometimes if he went to bed early I'd text Stephen to come over and we'd get pillows from upstairs, lie around on the sofa and watch rubbish telly and eat rubbish food. It doesn't sound like much but if I was writing the book of my life those would be the best bits. I curled up on the armchair across the room from him. The woman on the telly was bent over the bin so far you couldn't see her head and shoulders, just her big arse sticking out in her expensive jeans.

'We totally should! No one round here eats croissants – I bet Tesco's bins are full of them every night!'

'Wise up, Stephen, *you* don't eat croissants.'

'I could!' He shoved a handful of crisps in his mouth. 'I so could eat croissants. They're lovely. I had one on holiday last year.'

'In Scotland?'

'They do have croissants in Scotland, you know!'

He stuck out his tongue and I giggled.

'I just can't imagine you having croissants for breakfast,' I said. 'Bag of crisps, can of Red Bull and a croissant from Tesco's bins? Pure class!'

He threw a pillow.

'You're a reverse snob, Noll! You're afraid of croissants! You're bread-ist!'

I threw the pillow back and it knocked the crisps out of his hand. He shrieked and jumped off the sofa to rescue them. I was almost crying with laughter by that stage.

'Sure we can always head down to Tesco's bins to get some more!' I said. 'Are you coming? They might have caviar and frogs' legs too – no one eats them round here either!'

Sitting on the floor of the kids' church room I wondered what was really in those bins. It seemed sad to think about it, like a joke gone wrong.

Obviously if I was trying to hide I couldn't very well go walking around the town every night but I thought maybe I could do it once in a while, if I was really careful. And if someone found me then I'd only be back where I was before, at home, which is where I was going to end up if I did nothing. I sat for a while, thinking and thinking about the bins at Tesco and the people who worked there tipping all that food out. It wasn't far from here to there. Surely I could manage it without being seen?

Tesco was just over the road a bit. It's one of the things I like about Belfast. From my bedroom you could look out and if you kept your eyes at a certain angle, looking over the tops of the houses and churches, you could pretend it was just you and Cave

Hill and the sky making its shadows and the odd rainbow. But if you needed to you could shift your eyes to the houses and see loads of people going about their lives – women whacking clouds of dust from their doormats on the back step, kids playing with the empty bins on bin day, jumping into them and wheeling each other round, or kicking their ball again and again and again on the old lady next door's back door until she came out with her brush and gave them a mouthful.

It wasn't far to anywhere – Cave Hill was a lot further than you'd normally want to walk but you could get a bus – and Stephen's house was right there a couple of streets away – and this place – and Tesco. Although we never made it out to the hill very often, it was mostly each other's houses and Tesco.

I hauled myself up, still heavy with sleep but my head was clear. My stomach moaned as I got up and made my way to the stairway that led up to the outside. The light underneath the door was gone now and I felt my way again to the top. I put my hand to the door and for a second I almost changed my mind. It felt like going backwards when I'd come so far. But I'd decided. The door gently opened onto the night and I stood looking at the graves in the dim light. No one here but them and me, I thought. I kept close to the walls of the church as I moved to the front of the building but I didn't have to worry. The night was silent apart from the hush of the wind through the half-naked trees.

I began to walk, sticking close to the hedges. The street was lonely with everyone boxed away in their houses. I thought of Dad and wondered if he'd noticed I was gone. I thought of Stephen. I thought of the baby boxed away inside me. I walked past a streetlight that blinked and hummed and a bony cat curled up under a hedge meowed as I passed. A few more steps and I could get off the road. When Tesco used to be a waste ground Ciara and I would take this short cut for a change of scenery – somewhere else to play. It used to be empty apart from bits of broken glass and weeds. It could be whatever you wanted – a racetrack, a jungle, often a battleground if the other kids were out. It made me want to laugh, the thought of Ciara and me taking on those other kids. The amount of times we went home, our knees streaming with blood and our faces covered in muck. I lost touch with her when we left the Primary and went to different schools. She doesn't even talk to me now. I wish I had a picture of her back then with ripped jeans and her red hair falling out of a loose pony tail. Her posh friends wouldn't believe it.

Keeping my eyes down I followed the butts of cigarette ends half swallowed by the cracks in the pavement until I came to the gate hidden beneath ivy. Beyond it, a lane of flattened grass, worn down over the summer by kids who'd come this way with their flash lamps and big plastic bottles of cider. There were still a few empty bottles in the grass. Now it was a lonely path, silver in the moonlight with rain. I tramped across feeling glad I'd bothered taking the time to put my boots on that morning. Had it only been a few hours ago? So strange to have all this quietness. Maybe that's why the day had seemed longer. Hours and hours of silence when normally you'd be lucky to get five minutes of peace in the library before some kids came screaming in. Belfast didn't *do* quiet really but I'd had a load of it today.

The grass path was coming to an end and up ahead a floodlit structure was reaching up above the trees like a giant fortress. I sped up through the trees and squeezed through the gap in the fence, still there from when we were kids, and then I was in the car park.

I pulled up my hood, noticing the CCTV cameras that were watching random trolleys glowing like skeleton carts in the white floodlights. I'd have to be quick. I spotted the bins, but before I could make my way across I saw something else that made my breath jam.

It was him – the guy from this morning – the one who'd robbed my bag. I was sure it was him. Tall. Black coat, hood up. He had his back to me, spray painting something on the wall. I mashed myself against the fence hoping he wouldn't turn around. I wanted to run back across the path, but I couldn't turn around. He had frozen me again. I couldn't take my eyes off him. I tried to breathe silently through my nose. My bag! Oh my God, it was lying on the ground beside him. The blood pulsed in my ears. Don't turn around. Please don't turn around. I have nothing else for you. Nothing you need.

He was totally engrossed in his task; spraying the paint so slowly. It was like watching someone in slow motion, and he wasn't making a picture, he was writing something, but not in graffiti writing, just normal writing, so carefully, like he wasn't bothered about the CCTV at all. I could hear the ssssshhhhhh of the paint. Maybe if you have a knife, even a crap one, it makes you feel invincible, like you can do anything or write anything on any wall. But I didn't care about what he was doing really, all I could think of was staying quiet, staying hidden, willing him to hurry up and finish and then wander off leaving my bag. Was the food still in it? And my jumper? I shivered and it went from my legs right up to my head and I felt a bit dizzy. Sitting up against the fence I hugged my knees and it made me feel a bit better, but hurry up, I thought, hurry the hell up and write your stupid message and get out of here. Don't look at me. Please don't look.

That was when he turned round. His hood was up and I couldn't see him properly but I knew he'd seen me. I gripped my legs as tight as I could, trying to stay as still as stone, as if he could mistake me for something else – a shadow, or something dead. Please go away. I wondered where his knife was. I wondered if the contents of my bag had satisfied him. I wondered if he would care that I needed what was inside me more than anything. Please go away.

He stood there for a couple of seconds before gently setting down his spray can and standing up straight again. And then he left. He walked off, slowly. I let out my breath and when it came out it made a noise like a terrified sigh. I stayed there, shaking, for another couple of minutes before the pins and needles in my feet started to really hurt and I had to stand up. He definitely seemed to have gone. No sign of movement or noise. And he'd left his cans of paint, and my bag.

I waited for a few more seconds to make sure, and then I ran to grab the bag, bringing it back to my place by the fence, as if I was somehow hidden there. I emptied out the bag. Wallet gone, but that was no surprise. As soon as I saw them my whole body relaxed. Thank God. I ripped open the packet of biscuits and shoved two in my mouth at once, hardly tasting them. The sugar rush was instant and I wanted to laugh out loud. I sat down properly, cross-legged, and took my time over the next three before emptying out the rest of my bag. The rest of the food was there too. And my green jumper and the t-shirts. I put everything on over the clothes I was already wearing. You don't realise how cold you are sometimes until you put more clothes on. The last thing to fall out of the bag was my phone. I looked at it for a bit. It was switched off. I put it back in the bag with the other stuff. I could do what I came to do now.

As I stood up to make my way over to the bins I saw the message that the tall guy had written on the wall.

DONT WORRY – EVRYTHINGS GONA BE ALRIGHT

He'd been listening to Mum's CD. Scumbag. He was probably laughing at me and my crap gear as he was writing it. Still, I'd got my stuff back, I was about to find some food, I felt light again, like I'd fallen down a load of stairs but started climbing back up.

8

Stephen

I braced myself as I walked through the green gates. When I was a kid these Christians used to come round to our school once a week. They used to tell everyone how you'd go to hell if you didn't make Jesus your best friend. I was never that into it (who needs friends like that, right?). But the ones that came into school used to make you do this thing – they called it 'putting on the armour of God'. They'd make us stand up and act out putting on an invisible suit of armour: the belt of truth and the helmet of salvation ... it was bonkers, but it was meant to prepare you for tough times. So walking through the park gates I imagined my own invisible armour: the armour of Steve. I tried to think of things that made me feel like I'd be OK after this was all over. The belt of Nirvana, Unplugged. Things that made my life worthwhile. The breastplate of Feeding the Ducks with Janie at the Weekend. Things that made me laugh. The helmet of Nollaig.

Where the hell was she, though?

Maybe I'd go and see her later. I never called for her out of the blue, even though we lived near to one another. I always texted first. She didn't like people calling round because you could never tell what way her da was going to be. She didn't like people seeing him when he was in a bad way. On days like that she'd always come over to mine, or we'd meet somewhere else like round the back of Tesco. But I needed to see her today. She always cheered me up. I suppose I should have been worried about her, what with her da being the way he was, and her having not texted me all day. But I wasn't very worried really. Noll had always been able to take care of herself.

Mark was waiting there, just like in my daydream, sitting on the bench in front of the roses. But his face was different. Frozen. He didn't even smile at me when I said 'All right, Mark?' as I sat down beside him.

'Hi,' he replied, barely meeting my eyes. His hands were stuffed into the pockets of his black school trousers, his legs stretched out in front of him so that his body was barely bent in the middle. I just wanted him to say it – get it over with – but I knew what was coming and that this would be the last time we sat this close together, so I didn't say anything. Instead, I tried to take it all in so that I could remember it, the way I do when I'm studying something to paint. It was freezing and the handful of roses that had survived the frost looked brittle, like the lightest touch would make their pink glass petals shatter to the ground. A robin was hopping in between the plants, pecking on the hard soil, hoping to find a crack in the surface.

Clouds of warm breath streamed from Mark's mouth and

nose. His face glowed underneath a black beanie. A thin scarf, wound around his neck, doing nothing to protect his body from the icy air between us. He wasn't wearing a coat or his blazer. Nobody was wearing blazers or coats at the minute. Pretty stupid fashion craze to start in the middle of winter. But what did I know? Nollaig said she liked me because I had my own style and I wasn't worried about being part of the hipster clique. But, truth be told, it was a bit lonely sometimes, having your own style, especially when your best mate was nowhere to be found. I was sitting there thinking about being cool and being cold, and that's when he said it.

'It's over.'

Just like that.

'I know,' I said. I'd known it for ages, but it didn't stop the words hitting me like a brick in the face. I hate how I look when I'm upset. That moment when you can feel your mouth turning and you can't stop it. Noll always tries to make me laugh when she sees it going. She can't bear anyone getting upset. 'What's up with you, gurny gub?' she'll say. 'You look like you've been run over by a lorry fulla sorry.' I smiled, thinking of it, even though I could feel the tears stinging my face. Mark was looking at me. He tutted, like I was making a big drama out of nothing.

'Well, I'm sorry,' he said. He didn't sound sorry. 'But, y'know, it just wasn't working, or whatever, so ... sorry.'

'That's OK,' I said, even though it wasn't remotely OK.

'OK. Well, see you around then.'

He got up and walked off through the old green gates and I sat there and forced myself to watch him go, made myself stay and not follow him and not be pathetic and call out 'Don't leave!' or anything like that. I tried to think about everything bad that was leaving with him – the way he ignored me when he was with his mates, the way he snorted with laughter when he was looking through my iPod, as if my music was something that a three-year-old might listen to, the way he turned his nose up at our messy kitchen when my mum offered him a coffee, and the look on his face when Janie started yelling for a drink, like he couldn't get out of there quick enough.

But all I could think of was how I'd miss having him around, when he was around. How when we were alone, completely alone, he'd tell me the things that made him sad and happy, how he'd hold my hand ... He was different those times.

I sat by the frozen flowers for ages thinking the same things over and over, and then it got dark and I took out my phone again. I was going to text her one last time, and then she could go to hell. Maybe she was walking out on me too.

'Well, Mark finally dumped me.'

I couldn't think of anything else to say. She hated Mark, but she knew how I felt about him. If she didn't get back to me now I'd know that she wasn't really the kind of friend I needed. I wasn't going to text her again, that was for sure.

9

Nollaig

I hadn't counted on them locking the bins. Beats me why Tesco would care if people nicked their rubbish, but apparently they do. All that risk for nothing. They wouldn't budge. There weren't any visible locks but they must have some kind of mechanism inside them that keeps them shut or something. There were five of them, all the same, like huge metal lunch boxes on wheels. I heaved and heaved but it was like an invisible elephant was sitting on the top. Useless. I gave the rusty box a giant kick and regretted it instantly. It made a loud, dull noise and something big darted out from beneath it. I cried out and it whipped itself into the bushes. A fox maybe. My voice surprised me, it was high pitched, like a little girl, and I felt stupid for having made so much noise and having nothing to even show for it.

Back in the crypt I sat down at a tiny kids' table and cried. The low growl started again. Even my body wasn't on my side. I started thinking that if someone came in my stomach would give me away, even if I was well hidden. I got up to go to my busted sofa. For what seemed like forever I sat there trying to get to sleep. I was knackered and it was dark enough and at least I was warmer now, but it was no use. Every time I tried to swipe away thoughts about Stephen and Dad and the baby, they crept back in. Dad. What dad? I was an orphan really. The dad who taught me to ride my bike in the reccy was dead, as dead as my mum. It was like they'd died together, and left me with this dark shadow man who just wanted to hurt me and himself.

'You're not like her,' he told me one time when I'd stayed out all night, 'you're not good, like her. You're like me. Messed up, and stupid.' I'd told him to fuck off and he whacked me – boom – right in the stomach. I couldn't eat anything for two days because it hurt so much. Stephen noticed, of course, because I kept wincing every time I needed to sit down or stand up.

'Come on, Noll. I'll take you to the hospital, we can go at lunchtime – nobody'll even know.'

But I knew nothing was really wrong. It just hurt a lot and then sooner or later it would feel OK again. It drove Stephen mad that I'd never tout on Dad.

'Just tell someone. Let me tell someone. Anything'd be better than living with that psycho.'

But he was wrong. The funny thing was, even though I dreaded getting hit, you knew that the pain wouldn't last, and so it was worth it to hang around because getting stuck in one of those kids' homes would be worse – you get beat up in them anyway – or worse – and at least I knew what was coming with

63

Dad, and when he'd be most likely to lash out. You couldn't always avoid it, but sometimes I managed.

Couldn't take the risk now, though. And I knew that Stephen would tell someone if he knew I was up the duff. The only reason he kept my bruises a secret is that he didn't know about most of them. Good old Dad – always knew how to hit you where it didn't show – even when he was off his face.

I got up a few times and went into the kids' room. I tried reading one of the Bible stories books that were sitting around, but I was too tired.

I hadn't intended to look at my phone again. Part of the plan was to be strong and delete messages before I'd read them. I knew there'd be some from Stephen and I knew if I read them I'd cave in. I knew he'd be angry that I'd left without telling him, left him to cope on his own. He was like that sometimes. One time I skipped Tuesday morning History because we were having a test and he didn't speak to me for three days, well, except to tell me what he thought of me. He marched straight up to me as I was sneaking through the gates at breaktime.

'You total cow. I needed you in that test.'

I could see the rage boiling in his face.

'Why? So you could copy my answers?'

'You *know* I'm crap at History. And I always let you copy my Maths.'

'You're crap at History because you spend the whole time texting Mark Gallagher.'

He tutted and gave me the Look of Death.

'You *know* that's the only time I can text him because Finty won't catch on.'

So, Mr Fintan's half blind and that's why you're crap at History?'

'Yeah, that is why actually, but it doesn't matter because this is your fault, not his. Why are you being such a total bitch anyway?'

'Me? How about "Oh, Noll's not in school this morning, I hope everything's OK, I hope her da wasn't being a bastard again, I hope she's not DEAD or anything."'

He rolled his eyes and shook his head.

'Grow up, Noll. You'd just better hope I'm there for you in the next Maths test. I will be, of course, because that's what friends do for each other.'

'Well thanks, friend, I'm so glad you care.'

'I do. Fuck off!'

And he turned on his heel and walked off and didn't speak to me until the following Friday morning. He could be so stubborn. We both could. But it was worse to have a da like mine, wasn't it? I mean he could revise for his tests if he wanted to, but I didn't have a choice about who I lived with. Well, that's how it felt then, anyway. I think deep down Stephen knew it too, because it was never long before we made up after arguments. He'd come over the next day and bring a bar of chocolate or something. He wouldn't actually say sorry, but I knew he was. He had a temper, but it wasn't like Dad's. He'd never actually . . . well, I'd never seen him hurt anyone anyway. I used to get really pissed off that he'd lose the bap like that, over something stupid, when some of us had proper problems. I know he got some stick in school and whatever, and his boyfriend was just such an idiot, but he had a nice family at least.

But then I'd think about why he got shit in school. It wasn't fair. And he didn't have a lot of other friends. I mean, the hipster group let him in because he looked the part – kind of geeky but he had his own style – and he's really good at Art, but they didn't actually bother with him that much outside of school and you got the feeling they might drop him at any point. He knew that too. He needed me, and I needed him, and that's why we always made up.

And now I needed him more than ever. I thought, maybe I'll just read one message, to take my mind off everything, before I went over my plan and thought about what to do next, just one message before I had to start stressing. You know what it's like when you've promised yourself you won't do something because you know it makes you feel bad, but then you find yourself feeling bad anyway and you think, well, what the hell, I can't feel any worse?

I flipped open my phone and pressed my finger hard on the 'on' key. It sang its stupid little 'coming on' tune and while it was waking up I took two biscuits out of my bag and tried to eat them slowly because there weren't many left.

YOU HAVE 3 NEW MESSAGES

Crap.

NEW MESSAGES FROM:
STEPHEN
STEPHEN
STEPHEN

I ran to the toilet and threw up the tiny amount of biscuit I'd just swallowed. The air was freezing in the little cubicle and I gulped it down. I ran the tap and splashed icy water onto my face. Maybe this was the end. Maybe I'd just have to go home. Either way I had to read the text messages. I sat down again and looked at my inbox.

I read them in order. The first one had been sent this morning. I looked at the time. Almost twenty hours ago. Just twenty hours. It felt like I'd been away for days.

From: STEPHEN
Msg: Where are you? Are you comin in later?
10:05 12 November 2015

The next one said:

From: STEPHEN
Msg: Where the fk are you? Are you ill? Am havin shit day ☹
11:50 12 November 2015

My guts ached but I had to read on.

From: STEPHEN
Msg: Well, Mark finally dumped me.
16:29 12 November 2015

Oh God. Poor Stephen. Mark was such a loser, but still. I thought of him sitting on his bed feeling really alone. I didn't want to read any more. I shut my eyes and tried to think about Dad, lying in bed, not even realising I was gone, or realising and then smashing stuff up when he wanted food and there was no one to go and get it for him. I tried to think about the baby and how it was safe inside me and how the only thing that mattered was the baby, and keeping it safe. I'd switch the phone off. Stephen would be OK eventually. He had his mum and she was OK, she'd let him have a day off and mope about and eventually he'd realise that Mark was a dick and he was better off without him. And then I thought of him alone. Now more alone than ever. I put my thumb over the 'off' button and my heart lurched as the message tone sounded.

1 NEW MESSAGE
Shit.

From: STEPHEN
Msg: Can't sleep. If you're getting my msgs pls text back. If I've done something wrong at least tell me.
05:20 13 November 2015

Dammit. I had no food and no plan now. No one to help me and no way to escape. I was stuck and he needed me and the baby needed me too and maybe I needed them as well.

To: STEPHEN
Msg: Don't freak out. I'm hiding. There's a reason. So sorry. Pls don't hate me. I need your help. Pls delete this msg.
Noll X

Hands shaking, I clicked 'send' and the little blue speech balloon lit up with my message.

And that's how my plan changed. It wasn't going to be just me and the baby any more. Part of me felt good about that. As soon as I sent the message I started having this fantasy about me and Stephen running off together and being a wee family and being parents and helping each other out forever, the three of us, a unit, belonging to each other. We wouldn't have any money and maybe our kid wouldn't have good trainers but we'd be OK, we'd managed so far, hadn't we? And my dad would be far away and the whole past would be far, far away. Maybe Belfast would be far away. Maybe we'd go to Scotland where no one knew us and we'd start ourselves over again. The whole time I was thinking about it I felt warm. I didn't even feel hungry, or sick. It must only have been for about two minutes but I felt well for the first time since I'd left. Then my phone went again.

From: STEPHEN
Msg: Holy shit. Why didn't you tell me??? Where are you????
05:29 13 November 2015

I texted him straight back this time.

Me: Am in St Anthony's. Can't say why. Are you deleting these?
Him: Yes! Why the fk are you in church??? I'm comin over.
Me: Dont be angry. Wait till morn!
Him: It IS morn!! And I am angry. You totally freaked me out and I had a crap day yesterday.

Me: I know. Sorry. I have good reason. You have to wait till school time. No-one can find out I'm here. Pls delete!!

Him: FFS I am deleting! OK will see you in a few hrs. You better have a good reason. It's Art again today.

Me: I do. I swear. Bring food. Am starvin.

Him: You ran off with no food?? See you later.

Me: Long story. Runnin out of credit. Be really careful when you come – don't get seen. Come in thru crypt door round back. See you later. Sorry.

The fantasy was gone. It was double Art today – the thing he really cared about. Ever since I could remember that's what he wanted to do. And now with Mark gone it would be his focus – getting his exams and getting to Art college, without me, without us, I mean. The picture in my head of our little make-believe family crumbled into nothing and I was alone in my future again. Great. Never mind needing each other. He didn't need me at all. He had stuff to look forward to – a life. And no matter what happened to him he'd always be able to walk away. He was never going to be stuck the way I was stuck now. And he would walk away – without me. He was going to go off and make proper friends with artists and he'd get boyfriends that weren't idiots and he'd forget all about me and how I needed him.

I tried to shake myself and focus. He was coming. I should try to only think of now. I'd done something – the right thing, for now. He was coming, and bringing food, and maybe he'd help me somehow and maybe everything would be OK. Please let it be OK.

10

Stephen

The church? Of all places? Well, I had to admit if she was hiding from her da that was the best place she could've thought of because he wasn't going to look for her there. Nobody was. I reckoned nobody even went to that church except for a handful of pensioners that they sucked in by giving them soup after the service. Maybe nobody went at all. It seemed like a wreck and there were never any lights on. An old, falling down church. It so wasn't Nollaig's scene! She might've dressed like she belonged in a graveyard with her black eyeliner and those big boots, but I didn't think she actually believed in any of that crap.

I lay in bed, wide awake, thinking about it. Why hadn't she told me her plan? Maybe it was a spur of the moment thing. That'd be like her – she didn't like to plan stuff usually – sometimes she'd show up to school wearing new nail polish and she'd say it just took her fancy on the way past the chemist. Or that time she left Geography and said she was going to the loo and she never came back. But why wouldn't she have texted me all day? Maybe she was in trouble. Maybe the cops had caught her on, helping herself to something better than nail polish. I was sure that was it. She'd run off for a bit to give her auld fella time to forget about it, which he would do. He could barely remember his own name sometimes.

I rolled over and tried to sleep but I couldn't. My head was full of everything. Arnie and Craig, Jakks, Mark, my ruined Art project, and now Nollaig. I toyed with the idea of going to the kitchen and trying to find Mum's sleeping pills. But then I'd've slept too long. It was only a couple of hours until I could get up and leave the house. I knew there'd be trouble for skipping school. I wondered if I told Mum about Mark might she let me off the hook? I mean, it wasn't really a lie – I was upset about him, and I partly was skipping school because of it. Truth be told, even though I felt annoyed with Nollaig I was glad to have something else to think about. I knew it wouldn't work, though. Mum was obsessed with school. Mrs McKinney phoned home once because my RE coursework was late and she went bonkers. It was only a flippin' essay but you'd've thought I'd been picked up by the police for armed robbery. She was all full of questions: *But why haven't you finished it, Steve? Do you get how important this year is?* I knew why she was so freaked out; she'd left school with no exams and I think she thought that was part of the reason she ended up with Rob – he had a good job and said he'd take care of her. She reckoned if you could take care of yourself you'd be less likely to fall for some knob who treated you like crap. I thought of Mark again. Maybe falling for the wrong people had nothing to do with GCSEs. Maybe you can be smart in your head but not in your heart.

I flicked on the light beside my bed and grabbed my sketch pad. I could hear Janie talking her funny toddler language in her sleep. Maybe she could be my new subject – something innocent and good that could never get destroyed. I drew my pencil over the page, letting it remember what she looked like when she was born. This tiny little human – so wriggly and alive, and Mum holding her, looking so pale and exhausted, it was like the energy had gone out of Mum and into this new little creature, and the strange thing was that now that Janie was bigger it was like she was giving the energy back to Mum again. It was more like when I was little now – Mum smiling, laughing sometimes even, not taking sleeping pills every night. I hashed out a sketch of Mum and Janie together.

The alarm went off and I made myself stop drawing. I went downstairs and poured some milk into a bottle for Janie and by the time I got upstairs she was standing up in her cot grinning at me. She threw her dummy onto the floor and stretched out her hand for the bottle.

'Thanks, love!' called Mum from her room.

'No bother.'

I felt a slight pang of guilt knowing that I'd partly got Janie her morning milk to soften Mum up a bit for later.

Mum stretched, shuffling, bleary eyed, out of her room and into the bathroom.

'What are you up to today, love?' she asked.

'Not much. Art and stuff.'

'Still painting those roses?'

'Nah.'

The door shut and I heard the shower starting. I left Janie to her bottle and went downstairs to get myself sorted. 'Bring food,' she'd said. What kind of idiot runs away without food? I shoved some stuff in a plastic bag and jammed it into my school bag. I just hoped she had a really good reason for all this. We weren't poor or anything. My da had run off before I was born and I didn't know him, but I knew he was a cop who was terrified of his wife and kids finding out that I existed, so he sent Mum a cheque every month and that's how we got by. Still, we weren't rich either, she was definitely going to notice a load of bread and cheese going missing. I'd think about it later.

I tried not to meet Mum's eye as I passed her on the stairs but she was carrying Janie who was calling 'Steef! Steef!' and waggling her podgy legs so I had to look up and smile. I got changed as quickly as I could before Mum noticed the missing food, and I left, calling out my goodbyes at the door.

11

Nollaig

The first thing I did was check out the upstairs. There would be time to explore the crypt later and I wanted to see if I could find some candles or something. The stairs creaked like in a horror film and I decided I'd probably only do this in the daylight from now on. The stairs led to an opening at the back of the church. It was weird looking out over the dark room. Silhouettes of empty pews stood facing a lectern where a golden eagle holding a huge Bible on its back was blinking in the flickering light of a broken streetlight. Schools are just like churches, I thought, boring in the daytime when they're full of people, and scary as hell when there's no one around to fill them full of blah.

I walked down the centre aisle towards the eagle, every step echoing around the religious pictures and windows. One of the windows had a large crack running right down the picture of some old bearded guy carrying what looked like a big stone

book. I wanted to stand where you weren't allowed to stand –
behind the eagle, facing the people, telling them how to live and
what to do. There was a step up to the lectern and the Bible was
open. There was a bit marked for reading. The words flashed
bright and dark with the streetlight: 'Do not worry about your
life, what you will eat or drink; or about your body, what you
will wear.' I looked out over the huge words and imagined
everyone sitting there listening. How many of them would be
sitting there feeling like me, trying not to think about food,
trying not to think about anything? Probably not many. I ran
my fingers along the edge of the lectern and wiped the dust off
on my jeans.

I shut the book. I wanted to speak but I couldn't. I didn't
know what to say. I looked straight ahead and there it was – my
window – the one from the baptism when I was a kid. It seemed
smaller now but I could still see the colours, dull in the faltering
light. I got down from the lectern and walked towards it.

The great angel was still towering over Mary and she still
looked frightened but now she didn't look like a woman, more
like a girl. She had the same blue dress as the Mary in the picture
on our landing and a shiver traced across my shoulders with the
memory of it. She was Jesus's mum – but in the window she
didn't know it yet. There were words along the bottom of the
picture, 'Behold the handmaid of the Lord', and a brass plaque
underneath the picture that said Mary is being told that she's
going to get pregnant with Jesus. She has no choice about it,
she's been chosen. The angel had red wings and was holding a
white flower. It had started to snow outside and it made everything feel more unreal, almost like I was there and not there at

the same time – like the picture – dark and colourful but made of glass that you could see through.

I put my hand on my stomach and felt how it was starting to get stretched and how it was starting to curve out. The room was so quiet and the snow was making shadows on the face of the angel. It was cold and my head felt heavy with everything that had happened and all the thoughts that I couldn't stop. What is the point of all this? Why is this happening to me? Whose handmaid am I? And the angel looked right at me with its silver face and said, 'Your own,' and I felt a ripple in my stomach like whoever was in there was agreeing.

Well, that was it, I was definitely nuts. Pictures and windows talking to you? I imagined trying to tell Stephen. The look on his face. It was scary, how real it was, though. I was pretty sure this is just what happens to you when you're pregnant and stuck in a spooky old church and you haven't eaten properly for hours. Where was Stephen? I wanted him to come now. I didn't like the silence any more. I wanted noise again – kids kicking their football against the back door and drunken arguments outside in the middle of the night, the school bell ringing constantly and kids running around and screaming outside just because they could.

I'd had enough of exploring for now. I headed back down the stairs slowly, trying not to look around me. What else would I see? What else would be waiting in the dark? It was freezing now. I dug out my phone to text Stephen to ask him to bring blankets as well as the food but there was no credit left. I passed a high window on the way down the stairs. The snow was glowing as it fell against the navy blue sky. It was getting lighter. He'd be here soon.

I entered the kids' room and shut the door behind me so I could have the light on again. It's funny being in a place where you have no idea what's going to happen. I mean, even if your life is crazy like mine is, you still know certain things – like there's school every day except the weekend, and *X Factor* is on Saturday nights. But now I didn't know anything. I looked around the room with its horrible bright kiddie colours and scraps of paper and Bibles. This was all I could be sure of right now and I didn't even know if I'd be here tomorrow. And if I wasn't here tomorrow I didn't know where else I might be. There didn't seem like any point in doing anything since I didn't know what my plan was any more. But I had to do something. Clearly I was going nuts and I had to do something to stop my brain from completely freaking out. The door to the room where I'd slept was still slightly open. I may as well investigate it a bit more.

The first thing was to unjam the door. I squeezed in through the gap, closed the door and slid myself between it and the chair I'd slept on and I bent my knees and heaved my whole weight against the chair. It moved an inch. So heavy. There must have been something else blocking it but I couldn't see what. But it had moved a bit so I tried again. My back to the chair, I raised both legs and put my feet on the door and pushed. The chair had moved a couple of feet before this image popped into my head of a woman giving birth with her legs in the air. It made me giggle out loud and then I remembered that pregnant people aren't meant to be trying to move furniture. But then again they weren't meant to be fifteen or running away either.

Now that the door could be opened I could see inside the

room. It was a dump. Literally. In the corners it was jammed to the ceiling with junk. Boxes that had old books spilling out of them, something that looked like a pile of old blankets, a telly with a broken screen, three broken chairs on top of a massive old table that took up most of the space in the room. How did they get it in here? The ruined old armchair I'd slept on, a gas heater like the one in the kids' room and a big pile of old papers that turned out to be boring church magazines. The best thing was that there was a load of fat white candles in one of the boxes. They were brand new, someone must have forgotten about them. I'd look around the church for matches later, when Stephen was here.

Just looking at everything, taking it all in bit by bit and trying to turn it all into something good in my head, made my brain hurt. My stomach groaned and I looked around for my bag. A few Pringles left. It would do. Happy Breakfast, baby. I sat down in the doorway with my left foot on the door keeping it open and the buzz in my head disappeared.

12

Stephen

I could tell she was happy to see me. I was still a bit pissed off with her but it was hard not to smile when she looked so relieved. I sat down on a tiny red chair, the kind they used to have in our school when I was a kid. It felt ridiculous and I knew she was trying to keep a straight face. My phone buzzed in my pocket. It was probably Mum. I ignored it.

'So what's this about, Noll? I'm gonna get killed for being here, you know.'

She grew serious then.

'Did you tell anyone you were coming?'

'No. I won't. But Mum will know I haven't been at school.'

'I know. I have a good reason, I swear.'

She sat down on the other kids' chair opposite me at the miniature table.

'Well?'

She looked at the table. Something was really up this time.

'Did you nick something?'

'What?'

'Did you steal something? Is that why you've run off?'

'No.' She said it like I'd accused her of doing something dreadful, as if she'd never nicked anything before.

'Well, what is it then?'

It was freezing in that room. She sat there hugging herself, each arm shoved up the opposite arm's sleeve. I wished I'd brought more clothes. She was starting to worry me, I'd never seen her like this before.

Eventually she looked up and spoke quickly.

'I'm not going back. You'll understand why later. I need your help and you'll just have to trust me.'

'Are you joking me? This is serious, Noll. You're not going back? I'm the first person they're gonna ask about you. What am I meant to say? "Sorry, I don't know where she is but I'm totally sure she hasn't run off or anything so you shouldn't go and look for her." Something like that?'

'I don't know.'

She got up and walked over to the sink and stood there with her hands gripping the basin and her back turned to me. She looked awful to tell you the truth. She'd only been gone for a day but she looked like she'd been sleeping rough for a week. I felt bad about pressing her but she wasn't going to tell me otherwise.

'What do you mean you don't know? Maybe you should think about it, Noll. I mean, I've come here to help you, I'm gonna be in massive trouble for it, I had the worst day of my life yesterday, well almost, and you're—'

'I'm pregnant.'

Oh. My. God. Out of everything she could have said I wouldn't have guessed that one in a million years. The 'worst day of my life' seemed to disappear out of view as Nollaig's future filled the space in between us. A baby? What the hell? How did . . . Her shoulders started to shake and I could tell it wasn't the right time for an interrogation. My heart was pounding. I wanted to run – to just take off – to get away. Crossing the room felt like I was dragging my whole body away from the door and towards Nollaig. I had to not run. Not this time. I put a hand on her back. She turned around and as our eyes met she broke down. I don't know how long we stood there, her crying into my school shirt, me trying to think about what I was meant to do in a situation like this (should I say something? Or just let her cry? What if she got hysterical? What if someone heard us?). When she stopped crying the place where her head had been was soaked through.

'Are you OK?' It was a stupid question, but what are you meant to say?

She nodded but she didn't look at me.

'You've soaked my shirt.' It was meant to be funny, to lighten the mood a bit.

'I'm sorry,' she sniffed.

'Nah, it's OK. It wasn't my favourite school shirt.'

She smiled. Thank God.

'I'd forgotten. About school I mean. I'm sorry you had to mitch off. Everything's such a mess and I didn't mean to drag you into it.'

'It's OK.'

'No it's not.'

She was right and I'd've given anything to be there now. But how could I feel like that, now that I knew? God. Poor Nollaig. Surely I could give up Art for a day ... her whole life was going to be different now.

'It is OK. Can I ask you something?'

She looked at me and said nothing. She must have known what I was going to say.

'Who's the dad, Noll?'

She broke away from me and turned her body back to the sink again.

'I don't want to talk about it.'

'You can tell me, though. You know you can trust me, whoever it is.'

She turned around and looked me in the eyes sternly.

'I can't talk about it now. Please don't ask me again, Stephen. Did you bring any food? I'm starving.'

That was Nollaig. Drop a bombshell like 'I'm pregnant' on someone then ask them for breakfast. I suppose I could understand not wanting to talk about the dad, but my mind was racing. Who could it be? Someone from school? A stranger?

She sat down.

'So? What did you bring?'

And that was that. We weren't going to talk about it.

I put the stuff out: half a loaf of bread, three cheese triangles, three apples, two tins of Coke.

'Did you bring a knife?'

Damn. I'd forgotten. I shrugged but she didn't seem worried.

She folded one of the slices of bread and stuffed it into her mouth – almost the entire piece at once.

'Easy there.'

But she was onto the second piece before she spoke to me.

'Thanks, Steve, this is really great.'

'It's crap. Only what I could nick before Mum got out of the shower.'

'It's amazin'. Seriously. Thanks.'

I leant back on the little chair and looked around the room. It didn't look much like part of a church. It was all a bit disorganised, more like school. There were old books everywhere and the walls looked damp. What was she gonna do? Hide here? For how long? What would she do when the baby came? A baby. I still couldn't believe it.

'It's OK here, isn't it?' I tried to sound positive.

'Yeah. It's quiet. And I'm not on the streets, so that's a bonus . . . ' She didn't look up from her food. I'd never seen her eat like that before.

'Noll.' I had to ask her. 'What are you gonna do? You can't actually stay here and live off bread and Coke, you know.'

She looked up and rolled her eyes. 'State the obvious, why don't you.'

'Well?'

'I don't know really. I just know that I can't go back.'

'Because your da's a dick? Can you not just stay out of his way? That's what you've always done.' As soon as I'd said it I knew it was stupid. I just wanted there to be an answer. There had to be an answer.

'Em, duh?' She pointed to her stomach. 'If you think I'm

84

bringing up a kid with him around you have another thing coming. I only have to be away until I'm sixteen, and then I can get a council house or something.'

'Sixteen? But that's months away. You can't stay here that whole time. Look.' I took a breath. She wasn't going to like this. 'Noll. My mum's a good person. You know, if we told her—'

'No!'

'Just let me finish. If we told her, she'd be OK. Eventually. She might be able to help you.'

'I am NOT going back.' Her voice started to wobble. 'Oh my God, I wish I'd never told you. It was a mistake! I can't tell anyone, Stephen. They'll put me in that place that Lee Riddell was in. Or, like, a foster home. And they'll take the baby away. It'll be worse than living with Dad.'

'Chill! It was only a suggestion!' She was really upset. I tried to smile at her but neither of us really felt like smiling. I knew she was right as well. It's not like my mum could really have done anything. She'd just have told social services and they'd've taken her into care. And maybe things would have worked out OK, but like she said, maybe they wouldn't have. I looked at her. She had her hand over her belly. Not much of a bump but you could see there was something there. I suddenly realised that for once she had something to lose. She was shaking her head.

'You'd better not tell anyone about this, Stephen. If you do it's the end of our friendship. I really mean it. I—'

'All right, all right!'

I knew it was worse for her than me, but holy shit, what were we going to do? I wasn't just going to leave her, was I? So it was my problem too. Oh God. This was really, really bad.

Nollaig was unwrapping a cheese triangle and eating it off the foil. She lifted the other one and offered it to me with a half smile.

'Sorry,' she said.

I took the cheese.

'I won't tell. You know I won't.'

I knew what her da was like and I knew that if you were a kid in trouble you didn't get any choices in life. You had to rely on having good adults around to help out. I was lucky to have Mum, but who did Noll have? Nobody. So we'd have to figure it out. It wasn't the worst plan, staying here. It freaked me out to think about her being in a church of all places. But it didn't seem to bother her, and as long as she didn't get caught by some do-gooding creep then she'd probably be OK for a while at least. It would do, for now.

'Hey, have you had a look around?' I said.

'Yeah, it's just a church. Boring.'

'Really? I bet you haven't had a proper look. Come on, let's go.'

'I thought you hated churches.'

'I do. But I've never really looked around a church properly. Come on, I bet there's all kinds of crap in here.'

I didn't want to have to sit in that room all day and talk about the impossible future and think about how much trouble I, *we*, were letting ourselves in for. I wanted to do something fun, to muck about the way me and Noll used to. Just to forget everything for a minute.

'We can't. Someone might hear us. They might come in.'

'So? Someone could just come into this room too. We'll hide

if someone comes. We'll keep an ear out. It's a weekday and this place is dead. I bet no one even comes on Sundays.'

If I'm honest, part of me wanted to be found now. To be found and for it not to be my fault. Just to have someone else who knew what was going on. Someone normal, and good. But I couldn't break Nollaig's trust, I knew it was too important. I nodded towards the stairs.

'We'll be careful! Honest!'

I got up but Nollaig stayed where she was.

'I don't want to. I was up there earlier. I told you, it's not interesting. Let's just stay here.'

'And do what? Come on, don't be boring.'

I crossed the room to take her arm and encourage her to move but she flinched before I got to her.

'Oh, FFS, why *not*?'

'Because.'

'Because what?'

'I can't tell you.'

'What? There's something else you can't tell me? Bloody hell, Noll.'

I flung myself back onto the red kiddie chair. I was wrong. She wasn't boring. In fact I was starting to think I'd never actually known her before. All these secrets!

'I can't. You'll think I'm a mental case.'

She said it completely seriously but it made me feel like bursting out laughing. She scowled at me.

'Nollaig. You're the smartest person I know. You're the smartest person in the whole bloody school. And you're up the duff and hiding in a church. I already think you're a mental case. I mean, how the hell did that happen? Remember we used to talk about Jacinta McCartney and how she'd definitely have a kid by the time she was fourteen? And then she *did* and no one was surprised? But you? You were never like that. You don't even like boys.'

'I do actually.'

'Oh aye? Who? Who's the fella then?'

Her face was storming over and for a second I wondered if she was going to blurt it out and tell me who it was she'd been with. But she kept her lips tightly together. It was true, though. I'd never once heard her talk about a fella except for the odd famous person when we were having a laugh. She didn't talk about girls either, mind you. I suppose I'd never asked her about it before. And suddenly she was pregnant. Having sex with boys and I didn't even know she liked anybody! Why hadn't she told me?

'Fine,' she said at last, 'let's go up the bloody stairs then. Never had you down as a religious fanatic, but if you wanna go and explore the highly-bloody-exciting inside of a church, then let's just go.'

She'd said the 'religious fanatic' bit to annoy me but I didn't care. We needed to climb those stairs. I needed a while to get my head around this stuff. Nollaig was going to have a baby, and I was the only one who knew about it.

13

Nollaig

I'd just avoid looking at it. Easy. Like nothing had happened.

Stephen turned towards the staircase and I followed. Both of us walked upstairs without talking, past the little window where outside the snow was still falling in fat flakes that were gathering in a tiny drift on the windowsill. I was grateful for him being there. It was November but snow meant Christmas and it reminded me how alone I really was. I touched my stomach, willing the alien inside to move again, but there was nothing.

I thought of the words of the angel and then I thought of the words of Ms Laker: 'If life gives you lemons . . .'

'Hey Noll, look at the angel in that window. Look how the light's just . . .'

'Never mind that,' I said, 'let's go see what's behind that wee door.'

'What?'

I pulled him on towards the front of the church. 'The wee door that the vicar goes through after church. Let's go and see what's behind it.'

'You've changed your tune!'

He was smiling now, happy that he'd got his way. And I was glad to be getting as far away from that window as I could. And maybe we'd find some cash that Stephen could use to get me some proper food.

'Urgh, look at this place. It's hideous.'

He was marching down the aisle looking disgusted at it all – neat rows of dark wooden pews facing the pulpit, each one lined with little rectangular cushions, dangling from hooks on the back of the pew in front. For Stephen religion just meant bad people trying to control good people's lives.

He got to the door before me, marching calmly past the pulpit, past the altar rail, past the altar table with its long thick tablecloth and a small silver cross sitting on top, and over to the little door at the side behind the altar.

'The key's in the door!' he said.

He was like an excited little kid finding a secret passageway. What did he expect to find in there? Proof that there was no God?

'Come on then, are we getting into Aladdin's cave or what?' I offered a hopeful smile.

He smiled back as the key turned and clicked. Then he pushed the door delicately, as if we were in some kind of adventure film and he was expecting a skeleton with a dagger through its eye. It was pitch dark on the other side so we decided there weren't any windows, and turned on the light. The bare light bulb was so thick with dust that turning it on only made a small difference. Probably for the best. There was a window but it was behind heavy black curtains.

'Oh my God. *Look* at this!'

Stephen went straight over to the first thing he'd seen: a crate of bottles on the other side of the room. He took one of the bottles out and held it up by its neck to read the label, like he was a wine expert or something. He touched the label carefully.

'Wine! No, port. Oh *yes!*'

'You are *so* not having any,' I said, taking the bottle from him and putting it back into the crate.

'I *so am,*' he said as he lifted it back out.

'You can't! Stop messing around, Steve, they'll wonder where it went.'

'So? Let them blame the altar boys.'

'It's a Protestant church, you div, there are no altar boys.'

'Aye well. Who drank these ones then?'

'Um, the congregation? Anyway . . . ' I took the bottle again, 'I can't believe we're actually having this discussion. You are *not* drinking this stuff.'

He tutted, but he grinned at me.

'Just because you can't have any I don't see why I can't have some fun,' he said.

'What do you mean I can't have any?'

'Hello? You're up the spout, remember? No booze, no fags, no drugs, no soft cheese . . . '

'Wha?'

'Seriously.' He put the bottle down and started opening

drawers. 'My mum said when she was up the duff with Janie she wasn't allowed soft cheese.'

'Like the Dairylea you brought me for breakfast?'

He looked up.

'Oh crap. Well, I don't know, do I? I didn't ask her a hundred and one questions about having a bun in the oven. It was just one of the things she said.'

'What else did she say?'

'What do you mean?'

'About being pregnant. What other stuff aren't you allowed? I need to know this stuff.'

'I don't know, do I?' He had this look on his face like I'd asked him to run naked through the church singing 'Waltzing Matilda'.

'OK, calm down. Just asking.'

He winked at me.

'Here, look at this place. It's full of stuff. Come on, let's see what we can find!'

I had to admit, it was good to have something to do. We started to have a proper look around the room, opening cupboards and drawers to see if there was anything useful or interesting. But my brain kept returning to the cheese. Why soft cheese? That's weird. And maybe there's loads of other stuff I shouldn't be eating. Can you have Coke? I don't know *any*thing.

The things I knew about being pregnant amounted to very little. I knew how you get pregnant, I'm not thick. Although somehow it still came as a shock. Everything came as a shock. I knew it takes nine months to grow a baby and then POW you're a parent. I was trying not to think about that bit but it kept getting into my head anyway. I knew you got swollen ankles, heartburn, a sore back and you needed to pee a lot (I knew all this from TV and because our Science teacher was up the duff last year and she kept on having to nip out to the loo and sometimes she had to teach us sitting down with her feet up on a stool). I knew you got sick in the mornings for a few months – boy did I know that. But what I didn't know was that it's not just the mornings. It's weird to feel hungry and nauseous all at the same time – like you need to eat but you can't face it. And trying to hide it isn't easy either – people keep saying maybe it's a bug and you should go to the doctor and so you have to try and pretend that you're fine when you feel like if you eat anything at all it might kill you. I knew that you're meant to get weird cravings, like you want to eat coal or pickles out of the jar in the middle of the night, although that might be an urban myth or something because I hadn't felt like that. And that's about all.

Suddenly it struck me that I didn't know anything important like what you're meant to eat or not eat, or stuff you're not meant to do (like could you sleep on your front? Or curled up on a broken sofa?). I hoped that I hadn't made anything go wrong. How would I know if how I felt is how you're meant to feel? When I got that feeling in my belly earlier, was that a good thing or a bad thing? Maybe it was a bad sign? I thought about the angel and what it had said and again I was trying to put something out of my head. I turned back to the room where Stephen was up to his elbows rifling through the filing cabinet. I opened a drawer and it was full of pens and half-filled notebooks. I couldn't read the writing properly in the dim light: God. Holy.

Body. Kingdom. Another drawer had cans of furniture polish and soft yellow cloths that smelt of wood.

The darkness made the little room feel warmer than the main bit of the church. Having a door that could be shut and locked made it better than the room I was sleeping in. There were books everywhere but they weren't just piled up on the shelves. Some of them were being used. I got up and moved over to the small wooden desk where three books lay open on their fronts beside a framed picture of a smiling middle aged woman and two young kids – a girl and a boy.

There was a pile of CDs on the desk too. The one on the top had a picture of a pale man's face in close up, and his dark hair and eyes made him look like one of those emo kids that hang around City Hall at the weekend. I wondered if maybe the vicar wasn't the old bloke with grey hair and a fat belly that I'd been imagining.

Stephen had moved on to the cupboard. He was standing on his tiptoes reaching up to the top shelf and feeling about. What for?

'What are you hoping to find in there?' I said.

'No idea. But there's so much *stuff* here. Bound to be something interesting!'

But there was nothing on the top shelf apparently. He worked his way down, exploring every inch of every shelf, opening every box and getting more and more frustrated, sighing and clicking his tongue as he uncovered the dross of church business: a box of receipts, a book full of handwritten numbers and addresses, a set of dusty old hymn books.

Everything was dusty. On one hand you could tell that the

room was used regularly – the waste bin was full of scrumpled up paper, there was a black biro with the lid missing on the desk, there was a small vase with a bunch of delicate yellow weeds next to a card with a scribbled picture drawn in crayon on the front. On the other hand, it seemed like a room out of history – a museum room – still, like the rest of the church, and so dark. I wanted to peek out through the curtains to see if it was still snowing but I knew we couldn't risk being noticed.

'Come on, Steve, we should probably be getting out of here.'

'We only just got here!' He didn't look from his cupboard as he spoke to me. He was enjoying himself, rooting through someone else's stuff, even if it was dull.

'So what have you found out about the vicar then? Is he a serial killer?' I said.

'Nope. Boring auld fart as far as I can see. Not much here but books and shit.'

And yet he continued to sort through the cupboard. Then he stopped.

'Oh. My. God.' Stephen turned round to me with his mouth open in mock horror.

'What?'

I was sure it couldn't have been anything that interesting, he was just winding me up, trying to make me laugh, but I leant in to see anyway. He had his hand in the cupboard and his body was turned around like he was shielding me from seeing something really shocking.

'I take it back,' he said.

'What?'

'The bit about him being boring.'

'So? You gonna let me see it?' I tried to sound less interested than I actually was.

Stephen broke out into a huge grin and pulled his hand out of the cupboard. He was holding a bra. A pink, lacy bra with a pretty pattern embroidered in white onto each enormous cup. We forgot all about trying not to make a noise or who might hear us. I laughed so hard that I had to sit down on the armchair again and hold my sides, and after a while there was no sound coming out, I was just shaking and trying to breathe through the giggles and trying not to look at Stephen because every time I did he was dangling the bra or wearing it on his head, those huge cups – one over each ear so that he looked like Princess Leia in *Star Wars*, or slipping his arms through the straps and prancing around like an idiot. He always liked making jokes about religion or vicars, but they were normally the kind of jokes that made you feel like the person telling them wasn't really laughing on the inside. This was different.

When we had recovered I looked at him. He was still wearing the bra over his clothes, a big smirk on his face. It was like he'd won a prize.

'Well, I was not expecting *that*,' he said.

'Me neither! Here, do you think it belongs to his wife?' I said.

'Catch a grip!' He nodded towards the photograph on the desk. 'Does she look like the Ann Summers type to you?'

The lady in the photograph, with her neat haircut and neat children, looked like she might die on the spot if she'd seen what we'd just found behind the hymn books.

'A vicar with a sordid love life!' I said. 'Ewww. I think I'd rather have found out he was a serial killer.'

'Yeah. I wonder who the mystery woman with the big bazongas is! Do you think they do it in here?' As he spoke he was stuffing the bra with paper from the bin and adjusting his cleavage.

'Here, do you think it's a Catholic bra or a Protestant bra?'

'What's the difference?'

'I dunno.' He shrugged.

'Maybe one's more uplifting?' I said.

'Nah, they're both full of tits!'

We giggled at ourselves until, still clutching his fake breasts, Stephen glanced over my shoulder and squealed.

'Wha?' I turned around to see what he'd spotted. A framed piece of cross-stitch embroidery that read, in fine script, 'My cup runneth over!' I clutched my sides, tears streaming down my face.

'Oh my God, Stephen, I need to pee. Stop making me laugh!'

'What?' he said in fake innocence. 'Here, maybe the vicar puts on his robes for her!'

Trying to keep the bra in place, he waggled his arms out in front of him and tossed his hair back.

'*Oh Reverend Williams, take me on the altar, big boy!*'

'That's it, I'm gonna burst! Put that thing back and let's get out of here before I have an accident.'

I took a quick look around the room to make sure it wasn't obvious that we'd been in. We left and shut the door behind us, giggling like two small children. For a minute I was back in school, at the back of the French class passing notes to Stephen and trying not to laugh as he sent me rude drawings of Madame Lavine. I loved this feeling, the two of us being kids again. But as we walked towards the staircase down to the children's room I saw the window and everything snapped in two and I was back in the church, I wasn't a kid and I wasn't an adult. I was almost a parent and the weight of everything came back and I didn't feel like laughing any more.

'Jaysus, who ate your bun?' Stephen said, noticing my face.

'Shut up. And don't blaspheme.'

'Blaspheme?! Since when did you go all Mother Teresa?'

'You're in a church.'

'Yeah, and so is the vicar when he's showing sexy-bra-lady a good time.'

I smiled. He had a point.

'That's better. Anyway, what is it about that window? You keep looking at it like the monster's coming to get you.'

'It's not a monster, it's an angel, you dick.'

'You know what I mean. What's the big deal about it? It's ugly anyway.'

I rolled my eyes and we walked down the stairs.

Dear Lord,

Brian here. Maybe it's just the snow making everything
look new, but something feels different today. Later I will
go to the church and start making plans for Christmas. I'm
thinking of having a joint service between the two churches
this year to boost the numbers a bit, maybe get the Sunday
School kids to do a play. But I wonder if I can fix things
so that James Healy's father doesn't insist that he's Joseph
again. They're such a pain, that family. Forgive me, Lord, I
know I shouldn't feel that way ... *Challenging* ... let's say,
the Healy family are *challenging*. And demanding. They're so
demanding. Anyway, yes, please help me to be diplomatic, yet
firm, when it comes to casting the roles.

Lord, there's something else on my mind. I haven't
resolved things with Veronica yet. It can wait until the
New Year, can't it? As long as nobody finds out then we're
not doing any harm, are we? And I wouldn't want to spoil
Christmas for Alison and the children. I hope you can
understand, Lord. Just give us some more time. I will tell
people about her ... but not yet. I need more time. The
children are so young. They won't understand. Alison ...

well, I don't want to hurt her either. And the congregation. I know I'm not perfect, Lord, but I'm good at this job, and I know I am meant to be here, with these people. I knew it the moment I got here. I walked in and saw the angel Gabriel greeting Mary in that window and I almost felt for just a moment that he had turned his eyes on me with a message of similar intent – I heard his words, as clear as though they were being said aloud – 'the Lord is with thee'. And I laughed, because up until then I had been so unsure about it all. Following in my father's footsteps ... but I am nothing like him really. I never really knew if I was doing the right thing. But I knew then that I had come home. And now here I am, and I am frightened of losing it, frightened of losing my family, and frightened of losing her. And a little bit frightened of losing myself, Lord, because who would I be if I was all alone?

Goodness. I didn't quite mean to get into all that this morning. I shouldn't dwell on things too much, should I? I'm sure it will all work out. Please let it all work out.

Please help me to remain strong, Lord. I promise, in the New Year I will tell them. I'll sort it out. Give me a sign that everything will be all right.

Bless Alison, Jonathan and Clara, and please give Mrs McKinney relief from her shingles.

And thank you for the snow. It's lovely.

Amen.

14

Nollaig

Stephen hates churches. And vicars, and priests and the Bible and the Scripture Union club in school and all the holy kids that go to it. I pretty much don't care about it all. I don't care what people do as long as they leave me alone. Most people *do* leave me alone so I don't care about anything much. It's different for Stephen. He gets really angry when people start going on about the Bible or when some religious type comes on telly. I knew there was something in his past that had happened to make him so angry about it all, but we didn't really talk about his life before he moved here. I bet this was the longest he'd ever been inside a church. It's probably why he was so happy to have found the bra.

We spent the next few hours trying to tidy up the room with the big table in it and giggling about the vicar and imagining stories about him and his sexy girlfriend. After a while we got tired and sat down on the little kids' chairs again. Stephen opened a packet of biscuits and offered me one.

'What are you smiling about?'

He was sitting there, looking really chuffed to bits with himself. He winked at me and glanced stealthily around the room, as if there might be spies listening from behind the plastic boxes of broken toys and crayons. Then he reached inside his coat and pulled out the bra.

'You took it? You idiot, why'd you do that?'

'Evidence.' He grinned as he pinged the pink strap.

'Evidence? Evidence we've been in the room, you mean.'

'Evidence against the vicar. We're safe now. If he catches you we've got this on him.' He wiggled the bra and grinned. 'And don't think I don't know that you nicked a CD, so you can take that look off your face, hypocrite!'

'A CD? He's not going to miss a bloody CD, is he? His lady friend might just miss her underwear, though. You shouldn't have taken it, Steve, it was obviously hidden away really carefully. I bet he goes looking for it to give it back to her, and then he'll notice other things that have been moved or whatever, and—'

'All right, all right, calm the head!'

He wasn't taking it seriously. He still had this big smile like it was all a joke and he was holding his hands up in surrender as if I was deranged. I hate that.

I just looked at him. The Look of Death. I'd really had it with him this time.

'Oh come on, Noll. This has been the best thing that's happened to me all week.'

'Well, excuse me for not being entertaining enough. It's not as if I've just run away from home or anything. It's not as if I'm sitting here with a bun in the oven or anything.'

He went quiet, his face darkening.

'Look. I know it's not as massive as being pregnant and having to hang about in this dump. But things aren't brilliant for me at the minute either.'

He said it quietly, like he'd really been thinking about it and I remembered his texts from earlier.

'Sorry,' I said. 'So what happened with you and' – I tried not to say *Munter Mark* – 'Mark, then?'

'Thanks for asking.' I ignored the sarcasm. 'He dumped me yesterday, for what he says is the final time. The dump of all dumpings.'

Mark and Stephen had had this horrible crap relationship for about a year. One of those ones where they always break up but you know they'll always get back together. Mainly because one of them (Stephen) was so in love with the other one you know they'll always take them back. I was glad it was the dump of all dumpings. Mark was awful. He wasn't really a munter. He was pretty decent looking for a hipster – big floppy fringe and good skin. He was such a poser, though, he obviously thought he was better looking than he was. Urgh. The most annoying thing was that he seemed to have convinced half the school he was better looking than he really was as well. He was dead popular and Stephen had always felt honoured to be allowed to tag along with him.

'I know what you're thinking,' he said. 'You think that it's good we've split up. You think he's a total arse.'

'I think you could do better.'

'Yeah, with who? How many other gay guys do we know?'

'You don't have to hang out with idiots just because they're gay.'

'That's easy for you to say.'

'Yeah right, because I have the pick of the whole school.'

He stopped arguing then. I'd never had a boyfriend, not really. Guys do *not* go for girls like me. Guys like girls with long and very straight hair and very short skirts and very skinny legs. I don't exactly fit the mould. Guys like girls who laugh at their pathetic jokes and go out at the weekend and get hammered. I don't drink much, except for that one time, and I didn't want to think about that. When you live with someone who's permanently pissed you find out how ugly it gets. I never want to be like him. And I don't really care that guys don't like me anyway. All the boys in school are idiots, except for Stephen.

Stephen's eyes looked far away now. His mouth was a straight line, starting to turn down at the corners. I remembered that I was meant to be listening to his break-up story. I lifted the packet of biscuits and gave him one. His face brightened slightly. It was probably still snowing outside and the small glow of light that there had been from the window near the stairs was fading. He'd have to go back soon. I tried to concentrate on his words.

'I know he's a twat, Noll. I really liked him, though. He was all right when we were on our own, y'know?' I nodded. 'He was, like, really sweet sometimes and he was also the person I could talk to about Art and stuff, well, apart from you, and OK, so he ignored me if we were out with other people but really it wasn't all that bad. But now it's all over. And you're the only one I can tell and you're glad it's over.'

He wiped his eye with his sleeve. His other hand was on the table holding the biscuit and I reached across and put my hand on top of his.

'I'm not glad you're unhappy. Honest I'm not. You're my best mate. Yeah, I do think Mark's a twat, even more so now that he's chucked you, but I get that you're sad about it.'

'Thanks, Noll.'

He half smiled and shook himself like he was trying to shake the sadness off. He wiped his eye again and sniffed. Standing up, he ran his hands through his hair and pushed the little chair under the table like he had finished thinking about it and was drawing a line under the discussion and we were now in a new scene of the play, one where everything's OK again. How can boys just do that? But they can. I knew he was going to leave and I didn't want him to but I knew he would.

'I'd better go,' he said. 'You gonna be OK?'

I shrugged.

'Have to be.'

'You'll be fine. Tomorrow's Saturday and I'll call by again. Same time. If I don't come you'll know that I'm grounded.'

He saw the look on my face.

'Don't worry, Mum never grounds me, she knows I'll just huff with her and she hates that.' He smiled. 'I'll bring more food. Not soft cheese! And a knife! Give us a hug then.'

I knew it was rubbish. His mum was nuts about school and homeworks. She'd go spare. I got up and we hugged and it felt great. Warm and comfortable. That's what it will be like for my baby, I thought. He released the hug a bit sooner than me, just as I was wondering which one of us was needing it the most.

'Hey, don't be sad, it's just a few hours till morning. I'll be here with some more stuff then, OK? I'll try to get some warm things – a jumper, and a blanket. If you get sad, think about the bra! Think about the vicar running round in his pants, chasing sexy-bra-lady up and down the aisles!'

I giggled.

'That's better. See you later, OK?' He stuffed the pink bra back into his pocket.

'OK. See you. Don't let your ma find that!'

He winked and offered this cool smile. Sometimes Stephen acts so confident. I listened to him climb the stairs to the crypt door and then he was gone and I was alone and it was silent again.

15

Stephen

I was going to go back to school. I reckoned the walk there would give me a bit of headspace, a bit of time to think, and then I'd go back for the last couple of lessons, make up some excuse if anyone asked where I'd been, and make up something else for Mum when I got home. She wouldn't believe me and I knew the school would have already phoned this morning, and that she'd be rippin'. But at least I had a bit of time to think of something. The air was so cold, though, and the sky so dark. For the first time all day I could feel the night before – the missing sleep and the hours lying awake thinking about Mark – all piled up on my back, slowing me down. By the time I got to school I was wrecked. Everyone was out in the playground chucking snow about. Lunchtime. If I could just find a place to rest for a few minutes, just to get a bit of energy back. I looked at my phone. Three messages from Mum. I deleted them without reading. Twenty minutes left of lunch break. It was enough, and I knew just where to go.

Nobody uses the darkroom in school. It was built years ago, before digital cameras. There used to be an Art teacher who was a big photography nut, apparently. Anyway, he was gone and nobody used it any more. It was another one of our hiding places. A bit more risky than the place by the lockers because if anyone caught you hiding with someone else in the darkroom you knew you'd never hear the end of it. Mark and I snuck in there a few times. I shook off the memory. I couldn't let him torture me out of sleep again. Nobody about, nothing locked. It was easy to sneak in. I felt my way to a familiar space on the floor, underneath one of the benches. I took off my coat and tried to fold it up so the inside of it made a dry pillow.

When you wake up in a pitch black room it's hard to know, at first, if you really have opened your eyes or not. It took a moment to remember where I was. And then I remembered that I had forgotten to set an alarm. I took out my phone and the light was blinding. Another two texts from Mum. Missed calls as well. And the time –

17:34

Oh shit.

I scrambled to my feet. Oh God oh God oh God. The corridors were silent. The Art room was empty. Please don't let me be locked in. I looked out the windows. The school gates were shut, a big padlock shining in the streetlight. No cars. Shit shit shit. Friday afternoon? They'd all've left ages ago. Oh bloody hell. I ran to the doors but of course they were locked. The fire doors were bound to be alarmed. I'd be here all weekend! Mum was going to totally kill me. I didn't think I could scale the fence on my own ... Maybe she'd have to get the cops to bust in and get me out? I'd definitely be grounded after that. And what about Noll?

I was walking around the corridors, somehow hoping that there'd be someone – some teacher who didn't have a car, working late. I knew it was useless, though, they all had cars, and how many teachers had a key for the school gates anyway? Wait! I ran back to the window and squashed my face to try to see round the corner of the car park. Sure enough, there it was. The front wheel of a bike.

'Marty!' I yelled. 'Marty! You there?'

There weren't any cleaners about, and it could have been a kid's bike, but there was a chance that he was still here finishing off. For the next five minutes I ran like mad all over the building, trying not to fall on the stairs in the dark, flicking on lights where I could find them, yelling for Marty and hoping that he was here somewhere, hoovering or trying to get chewing gum off the floors. I checked the loos, the staffroom, the classrooms. It seemed to take forever and I almost screamed when I eventually found him. Top corridor in the Science and Technology block, standing there quietly moving his mop over the floor, like he hadn't heard me running around shouting his name. Thank God.

'Marty!'

He jolted and dropped his mop.

'Holy God!' He put his hand to his chest. 'What the ...' He removed his earphones and slung them round his skinny neck. 'What are you doing here at this time?'

It didn't take me long to explain. Marty never asked too many questions anyway. I think he knew I wasn't up to anything really bad, and he seemed to believe me when I said I'd fallen asleep at lunchtime. He said he was about to leave anyway and as he gathered up his stuff. How was I going to explain this to Mum? I tried to think of a story. Something believable. But all I could think of was how unbelievable this whole day had been. I couldn't stop thinking about Nollaig. My best mate, hiding from the world. She'd never been one to hide. It was snowing again. So beautiful. There weren't many beautiful things, but having Nollaig around, well, that had been one. And now what?

I walked to the student gate with Marty. He asked if I wanted a lift on his bike to my place. It was good of him but there was no point in being home five minutes quicker now, and an extra five minutes might give me time to think. The big steel gates were ghostly in the dark and I thought about the first day I'd met Nollaig, right on this spot.

It was the first day of third year. I was a spotty wee geek. You could spot me at three hundred paces; short, pudgy, ambling along with my hands stuffed in my pockets, head down, big mop of wavy brown hair, Nirvana blasting into my brains through neon purple earbuds. Not a target for bullies *at all* ... Yeah well, what can you do? It was inevitable really, I just didn't know how to fit in, never have done and probably never will do. Luckily, not being cool is now the new cool. Don't ask me to explain that, I can't. All I know is that sometime around last year it suddenly became all right to not be good at sports and look like a total nerd. Everyone started wearing these big plastic glasses, even if their eyesight was fine, and me, I started to make friends, at last. Well, not real friends, but people who let me hang around in their group – the 'hot' group. That's when I met Mark. But before that there was just me and Noll.

I had met her at the gates. That first day of school I'd walked through them, straight into the fist of Arnie Taylor. Nice welcome, eh?

'Where d'ye think you're goin?' he'd said.

I had tried to refocus from the punch. He'd caught me on the side of the head, whacked the earbud hard into my ear and I'd stumbled against the gate. I hadn't seen it coming and I was just trying to see who it was that had hit me and figure out what was going on.

'Nothin' to say, gaylord?'

'W-wha? Why, I mean, what's the craic?'

They laughed. There were two of them, doubling over as if I'd said the funniest thing ever. I started to think I'd actually missed a joke. I even looked behind me to see if something else had happened. But no, it was just me. I was the joke. The bigger one started mincing around on his tiptoes with his wrist bent over. He was calling to the other one in a high pitched voice,

'What's the craic? What's the craic, do *you* know what the craic is, Craig?'

And Craig, a short kid, was pissing himself laughing. I could see a few other kids rolling their eyes but they all walked past. That's what people do, because no one wants to make trouble. No one except Nollaig. I've never met anyone like her. She genuinely doesn't give a shit what anyone thinks of her. Everyone was walking away, towards the school, and she came running over from the main door.

'Oy, fuck off, Craig!'

'What's it to you? You gay as well?'

'Yeah, definitely, if it means never having to go out with someone like you.'

God, she had balls. Well, you know what I mean. I remember thinking why would anyone say that to a couple of obvious psychos? Don't get me wrong, I can handle myself and at the point where she came over I had gathered myself up and I was just about to explode. But then she came over, and it changed everything. Unbelievably, Craig and Arnie picked up their bags and gave her a glare before starting to walk off.

'We won't forget this, gothgirl.'

'Whatever.' She shrugged.

'And we'll see you again too,' Craig said, looking at me. 'Queer.'

She smiled at me, her dark eyes shining through a heavy ring of black eyeliner, and asked if I was OK. I didn't know what to say. It had all happened so quickly. Could I really have seen them off by myself? I don't know. There had been two of them and the bigger one looked like a right nutcase. She offered me a hand covered in rings, silver skulls, a Celtic band, a large purple stone.

'I'm Nollaig. Noll for short. Weird name, I know. The kids here are dicks sometimes. But you get used to it.'

We shook hands and she nodded as if to say *There. Friendship sorted.* There was a pause. We stood there at the gate. She stared at me with an eyebrow raised for ages before I realised she was waiting for me to say my name too.

'Oh. Em, I'm Stephen. What year are you in?'

'Third.' She looked older but it was probably the make-up.

'You have to ignore those twats. Arnie and Craig are the worst but they'll find someone new to pick on eventually.' I smiled at her. It wasn't exactly how I'd imagined making my first friend, but I was relieved to have someone already, and someone who could see off hard-looking lads with a few words? Brilliant! She smiled back.

Kids were still piling into school past us. Some on bikes, some with footballs. Mostly they were in twos or small groups. They looked happy, chatting to each other excitedly, and they all looked clean and new. If it wasn't for what had just happened you'd have thought this was a great place to go to school, everyone seeming so friendly.

'How come they didn't do you in then, when you interrupted them just now?'

She shrugged.

'I think they're scared of me.' She grinned. 'They should be. My da's mental.'

'Cool.' It wasn't really cool. I hoped I'd never meet her da.

'Not really. But it can come in handy sometimes, I suppose. Anyway, come on, I'll show you the best hiding places.'

And that's how I met Noll and she became my best mate. It turns out those guys weren't the only ones who were scared of her. Most people didn't bother with her and it seemed like that's the way she liked it. So when she told me she was pregnant I couldn't bloody believe it. I wanted to ask her when? And like, how? I mean, I know *how*, and you can't really ask someone *how* without it sounding like a massive insult, like 'Who the hell would shag you?', and I didn't mean it like that, but I couldn't explain how I did mean it, so I didn't ask.

I trudged home through the slush, trying to remember all

the details of that day. By the time I got to Hope Street my feet were soaking and I still didn't have an excuse made up for where I'd been all day. I looked at the row of houses. Ours was about halfway up, smoke streaming out of the chimney, and I felt like crying, realising that whatever happened when I got in I knew I'd be warm and whatever Ma said, or whatever threats she made, I'd still feel safe when I was in bed that night. For a split second the thought entered my head: maybe I should just tell her the truth. Maybe it would really be OK. Maybe Noll would be cross but she'd forgive me and everything would work out. Was I really thinking of her, though? Maybe I was thinking it because I knew it would make things easier for me – it would be telling the truth – a real reason to have ignored Mum all day long? But maybe it really would be better for Nollaig too? No. I wouldn't tell. I had promised. And she had been good to me – the best friend I could have had. I couldn't break her trust, after everything. I'd have to sneak out to see her, and I'd have to face Mum tonight, but it was the right thing to do. I walked on.

I turned my key in the front door, relieved, in a way, to be home. I could see the shadow of my ma in the hall. I knew she'd be ragin' and I knew she'd shout and there'd be a fight. But I knew I'd never be afraid of running into a fist in my own home, not these days anyway. So I opened the door and walked in.

16

Nollaig

That night I dreamt about angels flying around inside the church wearing pink underwear and I woke up with a pain in my head and a stiff neck. 9:10 a.m. Too early to text Stephen. He didn't get up on Saturdays until at least 11. The arm of the old armchair wobbled slightly as I unfolded myself. I couldn't spend another night crunched up like that. As I opened the heavy door the room revealed itself in the half light again, the big table in the middle standing rigid, a solid thing surrounded by lumpy shadows. It looked like something you could build on. A base. I could do this. With Stephen's help I could make this place feel OK, I was sure of it. It was freezing, but on the plus side it was such a dump and so quiet that I was pretty sure it was hardly ever used.

I slipped through the door and felt my belly brush the handle. When I was little Mum drove an orange Ford Fiesta. Everyone hated it but she loved it. She said orange was a spiritual colour and it made her think of the sun and that everyone should feel glad to see an orange car in the rain. Then one day someone at Tesco politely waved another car out, straight into the path of our horrible orange car and the sun was smashed to bits. Mum had a bad head and a stiff neck for weeks and we got a new car, a dark blue one, a bigger one that she could never park. She never got used to the size of that car. She used to say she hadn't had time to mourn the passing of the Fiesta and the big one always felt wrong. I wondered how many pregnant people felt wrong in their skin, morphing into a bigger vehicle that they couldn't park properly. Wasn't it meant to feel right and natural? What if feeling wrong was a sign that something *was* wrong?

My stomach heaved with the thought as I rushed to the sink, but it settled again. I put my mouth to the tap and the freezing water was painful in my throat but it felt good. I splashed some over my face and felt my skin tighten. There wouldn't be time for worry today, I'd make sure of that, starting with a list that Stephen had said I should make. Sitting at the tiny red table, I picked a black crayon from the biscuit tin and began to write on a sheet of lilac craft paper. I knew what was going to be first on the list:

Normal paper
Pens

What else did I need? I knew Stephen would bring food but there were other things. I turned my mind over the night and the day before and this morning. The darkness, my stiff neck, the thoughts that kept creeping back in.

Torch

Pillow

Sleeping bag? Something like that. A heavy coat might do.

Pregnancy stuff. I didn't really know what, but surely
Stephen's mum would have something from her last
pregnancy – books or whatever. Janie was still little and
the house was a tip so there were probably still things lying
around.

Last time I was at his house there was stuff everywhere, towels
on the floor, a pile of unopened letters on the table. I'd stood on
something sticky on the lino. 'Welcome to parenthood!' she'd
said as she noticed my face. The washing machine was whirring
away. 'Clothes and dishes,' she said. 'If I can keep them clean
and my head from meltin' I'll be doing OK.' She'd smiled a
slightly manic smile.

I liked Stephen's mum. She got stressed sometimes but she
was OK. She could be pretty hard on Stephen about his exams
and homeworks and she didn't take any shit but she was pretty
nice really. The house, though, that was a wreck. She probably
hadn't tidied up since Janie's birth and I reckoned she definitely
hadn't chucked anything out. I needed to know stuff and I
obviously couldn't go and ask a doctor and I couldn't just pop
down the library to go on the internet any more, so I'd have to
find out for myself, somehow.

I made thick doodles on the paper as the sun turned the half
shadows into objects. It would be another hour before I could
wake Stephen up without him getting pissed off about it. I
pulled my coat around me and took a biscuit from the pack we'd

left out. I didn't fancy leaving the room for another look around. Something sharp in my coat pocket jabbed into my chest and I remembered the CD I'd taken from the vicar's room. I snapped it open. My CD player was at the bottom of my bag. I untangled the cans as well as I could with cold hands and jammed them over my ears and started doing what I always did when I was bored and trying to avoid my thoughts. I clicked the 'play' button and started walking.

In Belfast you can walk for miles without being seen. Not because there aren't any people, but because nobody sees you. You zip up your coat, throw your hood around your head, put the music on, loud, and disappear. You don't look at anyone, you look at the ground and sometimes you look at the sky, but you don't look at people, and that way they're invisible too and everybody gets to be left alone. There are plenty of places to go but you're not going anywhere. Everyone will assume that everyone else is going to one of those places: the pub, the shops, the community centre, the hospital, the coffee shop, the chippy, each other's houses, school, work, the post office, church. You can walk to any of those places. But maybe everybody is just walking, like me, not going to any place, hiding from people by being among them. It's how you keep warm when there's no money for heating and it's how you stop thinking. You let the music do the thinking for you, let it fill your head. I knew that Stephen did it too. He'd get really cross if you interrupted him when he had his headphones on.

Anyway, I was stuck in this room and there was no one here to see me but it was still cold and I still needed to get out of my head so I started walking from one end to the other, tracing the shape of the floor space with slow steps. In time with the music, a slow piano beat and the low, male voice of the singer singing to his love.

All the songs were stories and I felt warmer as I paced the circuit of the room over and over. They were stories about love and death and some of them were hard to understand but I liked them. Stephen's always saying how I like this dark, boring music and I guessed he would hate these songs because there weren't any screaming guitars and no one was yelling about anything, but my music isn't depressing to me, it just feels like being understood. Even if you don't always understand the words, you feel like you belong to it and it belongs to you.

As the first song began to play again I remembered that, actually, it wasn't my music. It was the vicar's. Funny sort of CD for a vicar to have, I thought. Maybe it wasn't dark and gloomy to him either, maybe it was just his kind of music. Maybe I'd tell Stephen later how maybe I had something in common with our pervy vicar, haha!

Maybe I wouldn't, though. Stephen had really been enjoying having a laugh at him but it was more serious than that. He always talked about vicars like all of them were really nasty. I never challenged him about it because it was obvious that he had some reason for feeling that way. Who knows what had gone on before he came to Belfast. I didn't even know if I wanted to know. But I also knew that all vicars couldn't be awful because my mum liked Aunt Noll's priest OK.

Mum used to go to church with Aunt Nollaig. She wasn't really my aunt – she was my mum's best mate. It was sort of a secret that Mum went to Mass with her. It wouldn't have gone down too well with her Protestant mates. She told me about it when I was a kid; how Aunt Noll would sneak her in and act as lookout in case any of our family or friends saw her. After Aunt Noll died Mum couldn't go any more because she was too scared of getting found out. It would've caused too much trouble. It was brave of her to call me after Aunt Nollaig. It's an Irish name and at that time an Irish name meant a 'Catholic' name. When I was wee and adults asked me what I was called they'd give me this look. Sometimes they'd say something like 'That's a funny wee name, isn't it?' Mum would just tell them I was called after a dead relative and that shut them up because nobody wants to talk about dead people. Maybe giving me that name was a way to say that she wasn't ashamed to have been best mates with a Catholic. But she couldn't do much more than that in public. I knew that she still prayed and lit candles in her bedroom sometimes when Dad wasn't around. I didn't care much about it really but after she'd gone I wished I'd been a bit more interested because it was her thing, all the religious stuff. I wondered what she'd think of me now, rooting through a vicar's stuff and nicking his CDs. But there I was, letting the thoughts drown out the music, instead of the other way around. I stopped walking and took out my phone to look at the time. I could text Stephen now. I clicked 'stop' on the CD player and hung the cans around my neck.

'Hello.'

The voice had come from behind me. It wasn't Stephen's voice. I wanted to unhear it but it spoke again.

'Hi. Um, can I help you?'

I turned around. There was a man standing at the bottom of the stairs to the church.

17

Stephen

A row with Mum was inevitable. The school would have phoned her that morning for sure to see where I was, and now that I'd messed up the afternoon as well I knew there was no hope of her letting it go. Grounded tomorrow, I reckoned. For the weekend, at least. I may as well act like I was sorry; hang my head and give her some crap excuse about exam work being tough or something. There would be no point in putting up a fight over it. The best I could hope for was her being angry, me getting grounded, and her softening up a bit over the weekend if I helped out with Janie. What I hadn't expected was that the row was going to turn into the most massive blow up of the century.

I'd opened the door quietly in case there was a chance I could sneak in unnoticed but she was standing in the hall, arms folded, waiting for me. I wondered how long she'd been there. At first nobody spoke. Her face was a ball of rage. She had her bottom lip curled in and she was staring at me like a maniac. This was going to be difficult, despite the rehearsal.

'Mum. Before you say anything, I just want to . . . Should we do this later? Maybe it's not a good time?'

That was it. She was off.

'Not a good time? What time IS it? Stephen? Can you read the time? What time IS it?'

I took out my phone to check. Seven missed calls, from Mum. Four texts.

'It's . . .'

'It's five past bloody six. Five past bloody SIX. So I've been waiting here over two hours to ask you why you never showed up to school th'day. Do you know how much you can imagine in two hours? How many ways you can picture your selfish wee brat of a kid lying dead?'

It was one of those questions. Any answer was going to make it worse. I could hear Janie start to cry in the living room.

'And close that *bloody* door while you're thinking.'

I turned around to shut the door, relieved to get a break from looking at her murderous face. I shut it as slowly as possible to delay the row. Mum hated the neighbours knowing our business. It was one of the reasons we moved to Belfast – to start again. Even so, somehow there were people here who knew about it too. I suppose there's only so much hiding you can really do in a small country. I think that was the worst thing for her – people knowing what had happened to her, to us. Click. The door shut and I had to turn around and face her again.

'What the hell is that?'

I followed her gaze. There was a pink strap dangling from my pocket. Shit. Why the hell had I stuck it in my pocket? Oh my *God*. I couldn't explain this. Think. Think.

'I *said*, what is it, Stephen?'

I looked at her and my mouth was open but I couldn't make words come out. She reached over and pulled it out of my pocket and I swear to God if you could have seen her face you'd've phoned the social on the spot.

'What the . . . ? What the bloody fuck is this?'

Her voice had gone all high pitched. She never said *fuck* at home, ever. All bets were off. I needed to make it better. But how?

'It's not what you think. It's not mine. I mean, obviously it's not mine. But it's not a girl's either. I mean, it is a girl's but it's not . . . '

She was nodding her head in encouragement of the explanation that I couldn't provide and her face said 'Once I know what this is about I am actually going to kill you. I am actually going to tear your arms off.'

'It's not anyone I know. I . . . '

'You can cut the crap. You're a teenager, I know what you've been up to.'

She actually had tears in her eyes now. God, this was really, really bad. Her voice went dangerously quiet and she was looking at the bra, shaking her head.

'You know what pisses me right off, though, Stephen? All those people that said you being gay was a phase. And everything we went through, and now this. They were all right, weren't they? Was it a phase? Was it all for nothin'?'

Janie was shouting from the living room and Mum turned

her head. I knew the argument was over then, but it was too late.

Of everything that's ever been said to me in my life, what she'd just said hurt me most. Yeah OK, what was she meant to think, finding some woman's underwear in my pocket after I'd been missing all day? But it didn't matter. She should have believed me anyway. She said she always would. I felt my face sting the way it did when he slapped me, his ring that left a mark, his voice, hissing close to my ear: Repent and be converted, that your sins may be blotted out . . .

Even if she thought I was a wee shit, she should have believed me. We stood there, face to face, in silence for a couple of seconds and then I took the bra out of her limp grasp and started to walk to the stairs. Her voice wobbled as she called after me.

'You're going to tell me where you were. And what's going on. This isn't the end of this.'

And that's when I snapped. I turned around, towering above her on the final step.

'So ground me. Ground me forever. I don't give a shit!'

She charged at me and I swung into my room seconds before she reached the door. She beat it with her fists. BAM BAM BAM. So much for closing the front door, I reckoned the whole street was listening to this.

'Fine, Stephen!' she yelled, her voice breaking. 'I've been through bloody hell for you and this is how you thank me? Well, I've had enough. Find someone else to be your slave and stay out as long as you bloody want, I don't CARE.'

I stayed in my room for the rest of the night listening to her sobbing. I shouldn't have yelled at her, but mothers are meant to believe you, aren't they? Everything in my room seemed stupid and childish – the flowers I'd painted around my poster of Kurt Cobain, the pile of comics I'd been collecting since I was a kid, the framed photo of Mum and Janie last Christmas morning. Everything felt like it was mocking me – the stupid boy who got dumped, whose best friend kept secrets from him, whose own mother didn't trust him. Eventually I fell asleep with a pounding head trying to figure out how this was all going to work.

18

Nollaig

He moved towards me and I took a step back.

'It's OK!' He held his hands up. 'I'm not going to hurt you. You're not in trouble.'

Heh, that's what *he* thought. I'd never been in more trouble in my whole life. Standing in the kids' Sunday School room, looking at his kind, smiling face, I felt everything slipping away. I'd have to go home now. Back to Dad. But how could I?

'Now, now. Don't cry. I honestly just want to help.'

Help? Nobody could help. That's why I was here.

'Thanks. But you can't help. I'm sorry . . . for being here. I'll go. Just . . . don't call the cops or anything. I haven't nicked anything . . .'

I thought about the CD I'd been listening to. But it was still in the building. I'd only borrowed it, right? He glanced at my belly. Could he see it? I didn't think so. Not yet. I was just some kid lurking around in his church. This didn't have to be a big deal. But then he made this face, this kind, sympathetic face, like a sad smile, like he was really trying to care, and I couldn't help it, I burst into tears.

'I'm really sorry ...' I said. And I was sorry. Sorry I'd come here. Sorry I'd called Stephen. Sorry I'd even thought that I could really do this. Sorry I was standing there, crying in front of some stranger.

'It's really OK,' he said. 'No harm done.' There was a pause and you could tell he didn't know what to do. I started putting some things back into my bag. He was looking around the room.

'Oh!' he said. 'Did you ... have you been sleeping here?' His voice was soft and for a second I wondered if maybe he could actually help. I knew he couldn't, though. Unless God was really real and he was going to ask him for a few miracles.

'Just the last two nights. I was going to move on. I didn't take anything!' I wiped my eyes with my jumper sleeve.

He did his sympathetic look again and I looked away from his face.

'Let's go upstairs, eh?' he said. 'I'll put the kettle on. And we can have a chat.'

He wasn't wearing his vicar costume. He looked just like a normal middle aged bloke in dark navy jeans that seemed new and ironed and a thick knitted jumper.

'Come on, then!' He almost seemed happy about it. Maybe he was just trying to cheer me up.

He smiled gently and there was nothing much I could do. I followed him up the stairs. His feet clumped heavily and little melty pieces of snow fell off his boots with every step. He didn't look like the pervy vicar I'd imagined – a quiet, dark-clothed figure with beady eyes who preached hellfire and brimstone on Sundays but transformed into a lust-driven maniac at night, entertaining the women of the congregation in his back room.

As we moved towards his room, suddenly I felt the angel's eyes on me and I shook myself. Freaks and paedos didn't always *look* like freaks and paedos, did they?

'I don't want to go in there,' I said.

He turned around to face me. I was standing in front of the altar and he paused for a second. The lines on his forehead made him look briefly older and I thought about the cosy room. I'd rather be in there but everything seemed safer in the wide empty space of the church. I stood my ground.

'OK,' he said, 'I, um, I'll tell you what. I'll get us some tea, hmm? I'll bring us some tea, out here in the church.' His face brightened with the idea, like it was the greatest plan he'd ever made. I felt my chest tighten as I remembered Stephen and me messing around with what we'd found in his room.

'I'm Brian, by the way,' he called as he walked away. 'Milk and sugar?'

'Em, just milk. Thanks.'

What was I doing? I'd been caught. Everything was over. The best thing that I could do would be to leave now – slip out while he bumbled around with the teacups. I heard the kettle boiling. I should go – grab my bag and go. I could be home in an hour and Dad probably wouldn't even have noticed. I bet the note I'd left him was still on his bedroom floor, unread. I could go back, sleep in my own bed and get up tomorrow and make a new plan, start again.

The teacups clinked together and the vicar was whistling. There was a loud click and something began to hum. I guessed that he'd put the heating on. I should have left. But I didn't leave. I don't know what kept me there. Maybe I just wanted to see what would happen next. Would this innocent-looking chump report me to the cops? Maybe he'd give me the tea and I'd apologise and we'd all have a jolly good laugh and we'd shake hands and he'd let me go. Maybe I could get him to give me a couple of quid too, especially if I told him a bit of a sob story. He seemed the sort.

He came out, smiling through the steam that was pouring out of the mugs like smoke from two fat little chimneys.

'Mind out, it's hot.' He beamed as he handed me the tea. 'I hope it's all right, there wasn't much milk.'

'That's OK, I like it strong,' I said, taking the mug.

He nodded towards the front pew and we sat down, side by side. The heaters buzzed. The tea was still pumping out clouds of steam but I took a sip anyway. It was good to feel the heat on my hands.

'So,' he began, in the silence, 'what's your name?'

'Nollaig.' It was out before I knew it.

'Interesting name!'

'It was my aunt's. Well, my mum's best mate. She named me after her.'

'That was a nice thing for your mum to do.'

'She's dead.'

'Oh. Your aunt's dead? Or your mum?'

'Both. My aunt died when I was young. My mum died a few years ago.'

'Oh.'

The silence returned. Weren't vicars meant to be good at this kind of thing? Talking about death and everything? This one wasn't. I almost felt sorry for him. After a few seconds of staring into his tea he started again.

'So, Nollaig, what brings you here to St Anthony's?'

I was about to tell him. Everything. I was about to totally spill my guts. About Dad, the baby, everything. I wanted to. I wanted everything to be out loud and unhidden and all right. Now that it was all over he might as well know. Who was I kidding that I could make another plan? I should have left when I'd had the opportunity but it didn't matter anyway.

I took another sip of boiling tea and let it burn the roof of my mouth. I wrapped my hands around the mug and felt the liquid through the delicate china, scalding against the palms of my hands.

'Well,' I began.

'Nollaig? Nollaig!' A voice was calling from the room below us. It was Stephen. He was coming up the stairs. I turned around too quickly and some of the tea splashed out onto my leg. I jumped up and the cup crashed to the ground.

'Sorry!'

'It's OK, it's fine,' the vicar said as he jumped out of the way of the burning liquid. We were both in a bit of a panic.

'Stephen, don't come up!' I called, wondering if I could leg it over the pew behind me. 'I'll speak to you later!'

The vicar was bending over, grasping at bits of broken teacup. If he saw Stephen then the two of us would be in trouble. But it was too late. Stephen had reached the top of the stairs and was standing beneath the angel window, looking at us.

19

Stephen

Oh, this was just perfect. Not only had I had the biggest ever fight with Mum, but now I was sneaking out of the house having hardly slept, risking another massive fallout, and it looked like it was all for nothing. It was over. She'd been caught. No, *we*'d been caught. I knew it wasn't her fault really. She'd been the one who was so scared of getting found out. She was being so careful about everything. He must have just spotted her somehow. But even though I knew it was just unlucky I couldn't help how I felt. My heart was pounding in my head and I could feel the familiar heat rising behind my eyes. It was because of him – the vicar – his dopey face over the rim of his dainty tea mugs, all painted with pink roses. It was those cups that made me snap. I knew it wasn't her fault. I knew I wasn't meant to be angry now. I should have felt sorry for her. It was over now. But Noll and the vicar sharing a cosy cuppa? All sorts of mad thoughts were whispering inside my head: look at them! They're so happy together. Maybe they deserve each other. I'm alone now. He's going to help her and I've fucked things up with Mum and there's no Mark any more, and I'm alone . . .

I knew it was stupid to have those thoughts. I knew it. But I knew how things turned out when they started. I knew what would happen next. The rage. The fight.

Nollaig knew too. Her mouth was moving and she was probably saying something like 'Calm down, Stephen.' But I couldn't even hear her, I was so focused on the thoughts.

It doesn't happen that often any more – me seeing red. But when it happens there's no stopping me. I have normal, reasonable thoughts too. The ones that tell me what's happening, and that I should just calm down, count to ten, give myself a bit of space. But it's harder to listen to them because, truth be told, I usually want a fight. Don't ask me why, but it's true. Even though I know it'll be a bad idea and that I'll probably regret it, I just want to go for it. I want to lose it.

I knew it was partly because I was exhausted. I'd made sure to be up before Mum and Janie, gone round the house collecting things for Noll, trudged the whole way here in the ice feeling totally crap about that fight with Mum . . . and then I get here and find these two drinking tea together?

Get a grip, Stephen. It's only a cup of bloody tea. It doesn't mean anything, the good voice says.

But it does mean something, doesn't it? It means that not only is this over, but she's picked a side, and it's not a side that I want to be on.

I saw Rob's face in my head. His head bowed in prayer in the church, eyes closed, murmuring the Lord's Prayer.

When I lose my temper it's almost like I'm a different person, like in *Jekyll and Hyde*, when the doctor takes the potion and changes into a total psycho, except that's his own fault, he *chose* to take the potion. Me? I never wanted to be like this. The best I can do is to get out of the situation before I do any damage. Mum says that's progress. Some progress, eh? Running away. But that's what I try to do when it strikes.

That's what I did in the church. I didn't say a word to them. I could feel the tension building up in my chest and my brain starting to tighten up and my fists starting to clench, and I turned my back and stamped off, back down the stairs, making each step count, slamming my boots into the wood, hoping the stairs might break beneath me. Bloody churches. Typical for some do-gooding vicar to pretend he's going to help when really it's all about brainwashing. I'd told Nollaig a million times that vicars and priests only want what they can get out of people – usually money. And most of them are perverts too. As I had that thought I stuffed my hands into my pockets and remembered. I'd forgotten it was there. The scratchy lace brushed against my hand. The bloody hypocrite! He was up there, probably telling Noll that everything would be all right, probably telling her that she was a sinner for having done it without being married first, and meanwhile he was probably wondering if she'd do it with him too. Urgh.

As I was reaching for the door handle I hesitated. Maybe he really *was* a pervert. Maybe I shouldn't leave them alone. Maybe I just bloody *should* punch his lights out. It was all right in self-defence, wasn't it? And he probably really did deserve it. I turned from the door and let my feet carry me back to the stairs. So what if I hurt him? He probably hurts people every day. And he won't tell anyone, because I have his secret in my pocket, his dirty little secret.

And that's when I thought of it. The plan. It just came to me, as I reached the top of the stairs that led back to where they were.

The vicar was on his hands and knees mopping up the tea that Nollaig had spilled. His fat bum in Marks and Spencer jeans was sticking out the end of the pew. He raised his head above the seats and smiled at me. Nollaig wasn't smiling. She looked frightened. She knew why I had come back, or she thought she did. I tried to smile at her to let her know that I'd thought of something good – something that would help her – but my face wouldn't let me.

'Hello there!' he said to me. He seemed cheery and I almost felt bad about having been ready to smack him one. Almost. They're devious, church types, they try to draw you in with smiles but really they're all about punishment. That's what Rob had been like. Sunday morning in church, standing up to sing in his neatly pressed suit and combed hair.

The vicar stood up to face us. He wiped a hand on his trousers and stretched it out as he walked towards me. The cheek of him, expecting me to shake his hand. I held out my arm, letting the bra dangle from my hand. His face fell and he stopped in his tracks and lowered his arm back to his side.

Nollaig's mouth fell open. I thought I could see her trembling slightly as she walked towards us.

'It's yours, right?' I asked the vicar.

I could feel my mouth turning up at the edges. He was shaking slightly too, frozen to the spot. His hands hung at his sides.

'No. No, I don't know what you mean . . . what . . . what's going on here?'

But he knew, and we knew, and I was loving it.

'We found out your secret,' I continued. 'So now we've all got our secrets out in the open: Nollaig's hiding here and you're hiding here too in a way – with your girlfriend.'

The vicar's eyes widened, like he was genuinely surprised.

'What? What . . . girlfriend? I don't know what you mean.'

The thought crossed my mind that maybe he wasn't lying. Maybe we were wrong and the bra really wasn't his? But no. I looked at him, mopping his brow with a piece of the kitchen roll that he'd shoved in his pocket after wiping up the tea. He wasn't a very good liar. Still, he went on trying.

'No, you've really got it wrong. I don't have a girlfriend. I mean, I don't have a secret. And . . . and what do you mean you're hiding here?'

Nollaig was rooted to the spot. She glanced at me and her brow was wrinkled. The vicar had tears in his eyes and I thought I saw her head shake slightly, like she wanted me to stop. But she didn't say anything. I looked the vicar in the face. His tears didn't bother me, I just pictured Rob in his place, as if we were standing in Rob's church, and Rob was the one I was blackmailing. It was all the same, wasn't it? They were both liars.

One hand on my hip, I swung the bra around like I was the queen of sexy underwear, surveying my property.

'Nollaig lives here now, Vicar. Her and her baby.'

The vicar's eyes widened again and he looked to Nollaig who was staring at me.

'That's right, she's pregnant.'

'Stephen!' She was annoyed that I'd told him.

'I'm sorry, Noll. But he has to know if this is going to work.'

'Sorry . . . ' The vicar was rubbing his temples. 'If *what*'s going to work? What's going on here?'

'Well,' I said, 'we need your help. Nollaig's sleeping downstairs, and you're going to help us. You're not going to tell anyone, and sometimes you'll bring her food and stuff. We'll make a list—'

'What?' he interrupted, shaking his head without looking directly at us. 'No! Absolutely not. You really cannot stay here. I won't assist you in . . . what age are you, Nollaig?'

Nollaig was smiling now. She could see that the plan was a good one. A way out.

'Fifteen,' she said.

'Fifteen?' He mopped his brow again. 'You can't! I'll have to call social services, I'm afraid. I'll have to—'

But he stopped because I was in front of him now, right up close, swinging the bra back and forth in front of his face, a lacy pink pendulum, the two large cups swinging from right to left, left to right. The vicar's eyes followed them for a second, as if he'd been hypnotised. He reached out to grab it but I snapped it away and took two paces back.

'You don't want this to get out, Vicar. It'd be a scandal, wouldn't it? Worse than a fifteen-year-old being up the spout. It might even get into the papers.'

His face was red and I could see his worried frown changing

into something else. His fingers were beginning to curl in, the way mine do when I'm losing it. I was still swinging the bra but I couldn't take my eyes off his hands, which were turning into fists. The mild-mannered idiot was starting to look more threatening. I sized him up. I could take him. No problem, I reckoned. He didn't look like the sort that got into fights. But sometimes those ones can be the most dangerous. Nollaig saw it too.

'OK,' she said, 'let's calm down.'

I took two steps away from the vicar and turned around to chuck the bra back to Nollaig. His face followed the underwear and Nollaig gave him a half smile.

'You've been nice to me,' she said, 'but you can see that we need to do this, can't you? I don't have any choice really.'

I tried to keep my voice under control – not too loud, calm, but strong, like I meant it.

'Vicar, we don't want any fuss. OK? The deal is: you leave us alone. Pretend you don't know Noll's here. Get her the stuff she needs and leave it at the back of the church – under that window there.' I pointed at the angel. 'You won't even have to see Nollaig. She'll hide herself on Sundays. And in return we won't say anything about that thing.' I nodded to the bra, still in Nollaig's hand. 'And everything'll be OK. Right?'

His breath was laboured, but the plan was working. His hands unclenched and his face was returning to its normal pale pink colour.

'No,' he muttered, 'no. It's not OK.' His voice got louder. 'You can't do this. It's simply wrong. Nollaig, you need help, and I won't assist you in this, this mad adventure ... I can't!'

'You don't have much choice,' said Noll. 'I don't want to be in this situation, but you're gonna have to help us now.'

'She's right,' I added. 'There is no time to think about it. Sorry. You have to decide now. Are you going to help us, or not?'

He looked upset. Truth be told, he didn't look anything like Rob. He just looked like a slightly overweight uncool bloke who was about to cry. But looks can be deceiving so I stood my ground. After a short silence, he spoke.

'You can stay here. For now.'

20

Nollaig

I felt an ache in my guts as the vicar turned his back on us and walked away. It was a bad thing that we'd done. We were black-mailing him. And he'd been dead nice to me, making the tea and everything, and then cleaning it up when I spilled it. But I couldn't feel guilty about it. I needed to be here – away from Dad, to make sure I got to be the one deciding what happened to us. I had almost let us get caught, and now we had another chance to make things work. I had to take it. Anything was better than going back and ending up in that home all on my own, without my baby, someone else taking care of it, getting to decide what happened.

And we'd be careful – the vicar wouldn't get into any trouble, and this way he'd get to do a good deed, wouldn't he? Maybe he'd be grateful in the end.

'Come on, then,' said Stephen.

He started back down the stairs again and I followed him back to the kids' room. It felt different now, as if we owned the place in a way. We sort of had permission to be here now. We spent the rest of the day fixing up the little storeroom, moving all the books and crap to make a space underneath the huge table. Stephen did the heavy lifting, making me laugh by flexing his biceps now and again. I sat on the busted sofa and looked at the list of things I needed that I'd started to write. Now that we had the vicar he could be the one to bring stuff for me and the baby. It'd be easier for him to do it than Stephen. He could say it was for some women's refuge or something. It wouldn't even be a lie really.

It felt good, making the space look better, and it was great to have Stephen there making stupid jokes. It felt like this was the proper start of my new life. I had a place to be, someone to help me, and something inside me that promised something good. Something *actually* good. Not just 'OK', not just 'just-about-managing', but *good*. I pictured Stephen and me taking the baby to the park, pushing her around in the pram. Her. I knew it was a girl. I just felt it.

I watched him folding up a manky old tablecloth. He smiled as he uncovered the table beneath. It was made from a rust coloured wood and it looked old and beautiful. Stephen shoved the tablecloth in the corner, choking on the dust. I imagined us fixing up my flat in the future – making things better.

'What are you grinning at?' he asked, but he was grinning too.

'Nothing. Thanks for doing this.'

'Doing what?' he said.

'Helping.'

'No probs. I'm enjoying it. Lick of paint, this place could be almost nice.'

'Heh. Maybe Reverend Fancybra could bring us some paint,' I said.

'Hey, yeah!'

'Er, I was joking! Where would I sleep if it stunk of paint?'

'Oh yeah. Suppose.'

'And we'll not be here that long. A few months till my birthday. It'll fly in.'

Stephen draped the pink bra over the frame of an old painting on the wall.

'There!' He smiled as he observed the finishing touch to the room he had created. 'What's on your list then? Let's have a look.'

He came over to sit beside me on the sofa. I looked at the list. I had tried to be practical, thinking of things the vicar would come across easily:

Biscuits

Pillow

A book ...

'A book?' Stephen read.

'So?'

'Well, which book?'

'I dunno, do I? Any book. I'm gonna get bored here. Can't expect you to beak off school every day.'

He shrugged. 'Whatever. Here, that reminds me ...' He left the storeroom and returned with his bag. 'I brought you this.'

He reached into his bag and brought out a dog-eared copy of a thick book called *What To Expect When You're Expecting*. There was a picture of a happy-looking woman with a massive belly on the front. I took a flick through it.

'This is brilliant. Thanks, Stephen!'

'No probs. I had a look at it last night when I couldn't sleep. You'll need to eat better food than biscuits. It says you're meant to eat stuff that has iron in it.'

'Like what?'

'Spinach.'

'Wha? Get serious.' I felt my guts heave.

'I swear. That's what it says. Spinach is rich in iron. Put it on your list for the vicar.'

'Shut up, I'll puke.'

'Well then, put iron pills on your list. Don't look at me like that, it's a real thing, it says in the book you can get them out of the chemist. You need more iron if you're going to have a baby. It says so in—'

'In the book, yeah, I get it.'

He grinned. Maybe he was right. I scribbled 'pills for extra iron' on the list, hoping that the vicar had heard of them.

'What else, then? Apart from iron.'

'Meat. More vegetables. And fruit.'

'Yuck.'

'Well, you have to have them. It says—'

'OK, OK!' I tutted. 'Didn't know you needed a degree in health foods to have a baby.'

'You're the one who wanted the book,' he teased. He was loving this.

I rolled my eyes and wrote 'fruit and vegetables' on the list.

'Cooked,' he said.

'What?'

'Write "cooked". If you don't he might bring you a raw onion or something.'

'But I don't want a cooked onion.'

'Well, don't write "onion" then! Tell him which ones you like.'

'I don't like any fruits or vegetables.'

'Give me that.'

Stephen reached over me and grabbed the sheet of paper and the crayon. At the end of the list he wrote 'Bananas, apples and some other food – healthy stuff – cooked'.

'You should write "thanks",' I said.

'Why?'

'Cos. It's polite. And he's doing us a favour.'

'Er, no. We're doing *him* a favour, by not letting everyone know he's a perv.'

I didn't want to get him started about religion again so I said 'OK' and decided that I'd write 'thanks' at the end of the list after he'd gone. We spent the rest of the afternoon making the storeroom into my bedroom and fixing up the list, getting it just right, like a letter to Santa. When it was done and Stephen had gone, I took it up the stairs and left it in the vicar's little room, on the desk, next to his poetry books and the vase of wilted yellow weeds.

Dear Lord,

It's me, Brian, again.

I don't think that this was quite what I had in mind when I asked you for a sign. But perhaps you are letting me know that you are angry. That is fair, I think. I shouldn't have secrets. I know that. I know I should tell the truth. But I can't. I mean, it isn't the right time. I know it is wrong to hide the truth about Veronica and me, but I have to, because if people knew then everything would change – everything good would go wrong.

I know, I know. You're telling me to be honest and I'm running away. I'm Jonah and this young pregnant girl is the whale. Hmmmm, perhaps I could think of a less insulting analogy . . . she's not quite a whale yet . . .

Well anyway, I'm in quite a fix now. I'm sure that Nollaig is in more trouble than she's telling me. The poor girl. If it wasn't for that boyfriend of hers I don't think she'd be hiding here at all. I'm sure it was all his idea.

Anyway, I know I should tell someone. It is my duty. I know that. But there's Alison and the children. And it's Christmas. They don't deserve to be so upset at Christmas, do they? And my calling. I love my job. I'm a good vicar, I know I am. St Anthony's and St Mark's are small but they're growing. That's because of me, Lord ... I really think it's because of me. And it's not just the numbers. I'm helping people. Mr Palmer said that if it wasn't for me calling on a Monday afternoon he wouldn't see anyone but the home help all week. And not all vicars enjoy home visits, Lord. Some of them just want to preach, you know. I think some of them would be happy talking to an empty room ...

Perhaps I can even help this girl without everything going wrong. Perhaps she only needs a little time to think about things. Maybe I can persuade her to let the authorities know what's happening. Yes, I'm sure that's what I'm meant to do, Lord. I will help her. It's my duty to help her, isn't it? I know, I know, I should tell the authorities myself ... but I will help her as much as I can. If she's still here after Christmas I'll definitely tell someone what's going on. And then I'll tell Alison everything. I will. But perhaps she'll be gone before then and I won't need to tell anyone. I mean surely she won't want to spend Christmas hiding in an old church.

Please let her be gone by Christmas, Lord.

Please let Nollaig be OK.

Please let it be OK that I'm helping her to hide.

Please don't let anyone find out.

I know I'm a coward. But I need Veronica. I know that you understand that, even if nobody else does. I think I would die without her. A part of me would die, at least.

I'm so sorry. Please help me to do what is best, for everyone.

Amen.

21

Stephen

Noll's room looked great when it was finished. I left her sitting on the mattress we'd made out of a pile of old curtains underneath the table. Bit dusty, but it would have to do, at least until the vicar could bring something better.

It made me feel good, us writing the list. The vicar was clueless but I reckoned he'd probably get the stuff that Nollaig needed. The look on his face when he saw the bra! I laughed to myself as I trudged home through the fresh snow, crunching my soggy Cons through the perfect thick wedding cake icing on the pavements.

I didn't even feel worried about Mum. Maybe she'd still be angry but everything would be OK in a while – she was too busy with Janie to stay cross. I called into the garage on the corner and bought some Jamaica ginger cake. Her favourite. Maybe she'd be feeling guilty for what she'd said to me. We'd both said stuff we didn't mean.

And that's how it went. Red-eyed hugs in the kitchen, me sticking on the kettle, Janie, who could sense something going on, waddling around giving everyone wet kisses. It was over as quickly as it had started. Mum didn't mention the bra again and I didn't bring it up. We didn't talk about anything – we just said sorry. It was enough. Back to normal.

But how could I go back to normal? I knew a secret that only two other people knew. And now that Mum had found evidence and we'd fought and made up about it, well, it was like a double lie. I was hiding Nollaig and letting Mum think that she'd been wrong to get annoyed, when if she knew the truth she'd freak out way more than she did that night. But what could I do? I tried to put it away, forget about it, just get on with things. But school wasn't helping. After a fortnight or so I got called into Jakks's office again.

'Take a seat, Stephen.'

He looked grave. It wasn't until I'd been in the room a couple of seconds that I noticed the police officers standing at the door. Holy shit.

'What's all this about?' I asked. But I knew.

'Don't panic, Stephen.' He indicated the cops to sit down. 'These officers would like to ask you something. It's about your friend, Nollaig.'

The cops lumbered over to their seats. A man and a woman. They always looked so huge in all their gear. Each one had a pistol strapped to their hip. I knew you weren't meant to look at their guns but I could never help it. They could just kill a person, any time. Truth be told, it made it a bit hard to relax. The woman spoke first.

'We just want to ask you about Nollaig, Stephen. She hasn't come to school for some time, and there's no answer when we call at her house. Do you have any idea where she might be?' Her voice was soft and she smiled. She had blonde hair neatly tucked under her cap. Flawless make-up. I liked her.

'Em, no. Sorry.'

'You're her best friend, is that right?' The man's voice was more harsh. He did not smile. I could tell he didn't believe me.

'Yes, but ... it's not unusual for Noll to beak ... I mean, it's not unusual for her to be ill and not come into school for a bit. She'll probably come back at some point.'

It was so weak but what could I say? Why hadn't I thought about this happening? What an idiot. Jakks had his fingers steepled against his mouth, his eyebrows narrowed, and the cops were both writing stuff down in their notebooks. Was this evidence? How much trouble was I getting into?

'Calm down, son. We're only asking if anyone's seen her. You're not in any trouble. Yet.' The big cop smirked as he said the word 'yet' – like it was a joke, but I didn't feel like he was really joking. Everyone else smiled. I needed to get out of there. The woman took over.

'When did you last see Nollaig?'

'Em. I dunno. A couple of weeks ago?'

'A couple of weeks?' the male cop said. 'That's quite a long time for a best friend, isn't it?'

Smartarse. He was starting to annoy me.

'Not really,' I said, 'she's like that sometimes.'

He raised an eyebrow.

'And she didn't contact you at all during that time?'

'No.'

The woman took over without looking up from her notepad.

'The last time you saw Nollaig, how did she seem?'

'What do you mean?'

'I mean, did she seem OK to you? Happy?'

I almost laughed. The last time I saw Noll before she ran off she was flipping the finger to Arnie Taylor as she walked out the school gates.

'Yeah, she did seem happy. Why? Do you think . . . ?'

What did they think? That she'd done herself in? Shit. Maybe I should act more worried. I tried to put on a concerned face.

'Wait,' I said, 'do you think she's . . .' I couldn't say it. Even though I knew she hadn't done anything like that, I couldn't say the word. Just thinking about it I could feel my forehead going clammy. Oh God. These lies were fucking huge now, weren't they?

'I won't lie about this, Stephen,' the female officer said. 'We're concerned about Nollaig. We think there's someone in her house and they're not answering the door. We're going to go back later today. But it's very important that if you hear anything, or remember anything, you let us know, OK?'

I had to get out. This was way worse than anything. Worse than blackmailing the vicar, worse than lying to Mum. Was I breaking the law, lying to them?

'Can I go now?' I pleaded with Jakks. 'I'll let you know if I see Nollaig. Is that OK?'

Jakks looked at the cops and the woman nodded.

'Yes, you can go, Stephen,' Jakks said, 'and don't worry about

Nollaig. As you said, she'll probably show up sooner or later. We'll leave it to the police to sort out. OK?'

'Em, OK. Thanks.' I turned to the cops on my way out. 'Thanks. I hope you find her soon.'

The male cop took a breath. 'We do too, son. We do too.'

I wished that it had ended there but it didn't. Of course everyone in school had seen the cops arriving, and the rumour quickly got around that it was me they wanted to speak to, and pretty soon everyone had put two and two together and the entire school was talking about Nollaig. The invented stories about what she'd done and where she was were becoming truths and I couldn't do anything about it. Every morning at the lockers I'd hear new whispers about her: 'Did you hear that she tried to rob the post office and now she's on the run?' 'She tried to slit her wrists last year and she told someone she was going to jump in the Lagan before the GCSE mocks.' And I couldn't do anything, I couldn't tell them to piss off and I couldn't tell them the truth, and when I told Nollaig about it she was delighted because nobody had guessed that she was pregnant and hiding. It was a mess.

I kept wondering if I was doing the right thing, keeping it a secret, and the longer it went on the more trouble I knew I was causing for myself as well as her if we ever got caught. But she was determined; she wanted to be away from her dad and she wanted to keep her baby, and both of us knew that the only way to make those things happen was if nobody knew where Nollaig was. I couldn't blame her. The stories that kids told about the care home in town were awful. There was no way they'd let a baby stay in there. Most of the kids in there spent their weekends getting lifted by the cops for stealing, and loads of them were on drugs. I knew Noll could handle herself, but it was properly rough. Just a few months ago one of the kids stabbed one of the workers for trying to ground him. You could see why she felt she didn't have any choice.

So I tried keeping my head down, ignoring the rumours, focusing on Art. I stopped mitching off in case anyone got suspicious and I only saw Nollaig after school. But sooner or later I knew the shit would hit the fan. And about a week later, it did.

I'd come home from school via the church where I left Nollaig reading some boring church magazine and waiting for the vicar's next delivery. The snow had thawed and then started again and I kicked up the dirty slush as I walked, making room for a fresh blanket of white flakes to line the pavement. The air was freezing and it made my head light but I liked the newness of the snowfall. When I got home Mum was sitting on the stairs with her head in her hands. Janie was burbling away in her playpen in the living room, banging her pots with a wooden spoon. Mum looked up as I closed the door. Her eyes were red.

'Mum ... what is it?' I started. A death, I thought. Maybe Rob?

'What?' she mumbled, looking up from her thoughts.

Maybe he'd finally picked on someone bigger than himself. I was starting to stress about how to feel about it when Mum spoke again and I froze.

'It's Nollaig.'

She started to cry then and she got up slowly and put her arms out, her head cocked to one side, with this look on her face, almost as if it was her fault. She was saying 'Sorry, sorry' as she put her arms around me. I broke the embrace.

'Wait. What's going on? What about Nollaig?'

She sniffed and took my hand, leading me into the kitchen.

'I'll put the kettle on.'

It was like a weird dream. I'd just been with Nollaig, ten minutes ago. Even if something had happened within that space of time there's no way it could've got back to Mum before I'd got home.

'I don't want tea, Ma. Would you just tell me what's going on?'

'OK.' She turned around from the kettle, stood up straight and steadied herself against the counter. 'I'm so sorry to tell you this, Stephen, but it looks like Nollaig might be dead.'

Her voice broke again and her shoulders slumped. I thought she was going to fall over so I got up and led her over to a chair.

'It's OK, Mum. I don't think so. I don't think you could be right.'

'I know this is hard, son. Ah, look at me! I'm the one who should be comforting you!' She buried her face in her hands.

'Look. Just, just calm down a bit, Mum. Why do you think she's dead? What's happened?'

There was a tiny part of me that was starting to panic. What if it was true? But it couldn't be ... but what if somehow time had changed between me leaving the church and getting home and it had all happened in between? Think. Did I walk straight home? No! I'd been to the shop to get milk. How long did that take? Was the checkout queue slow? Oh God, could this be true?

'Mum. Please. Just tell me why you think that she's ...' I couldn't say the word, now that it was becoming a possibility.

Mum looked up and wiped her face on her jumper sleeve. Her eyes looked sore.

'She left a note, love.'

'What? What note?'

'Her dad said. She left a note. Like, a suicide note.'

What? Nollaig hadn't mentioned a note. Mum went on. She'd heard it from a neighbour whose sister was a classroom assistant in school. The sister had heard it in the staffroom and, apparently, the teachers had been told, just today, by Mr Jakks. I didn't know how much was true and how much had been added on to the original story, but Mum said that Nollaig's dad had been visited by the police because Noll had missed so many days off school. He was drunk, of course. They'd asked him if he knew where Nollaig was and then he'd showed them this supposed note that said she was going to top herself. As if Noll would ever do that! It made me angry thinking of those idiots in their big costumes believing Nollaig's pissed da and his rubbish story that he'd obviously made up to keep himself out of trouble. I bet if there was a note he wrote it himself. Apparently he was so drunk they'd just assumed he'd been too distraught to report it. How thick were they? He could've murdered her for all they knew.

'They found something else, love,' said Mum. She reached out and grabbed my arm but it was only to steady herself. 'Her wallet. They found it in the river. I'm so sorry, love!' She wiped at her eyes. God. They'd added everything up – evidence, a drunk fella's story, the rumours in school. My head was spinning.

I looked at Mum, drinking her tea in short sips, composing herself, wiping her eyes and sitting up straight, and I knew we were in deep shit now. I hadn't thought anyone would be really upset by Nollaig running off. People ignored her most of the time and if they didn't they were saying stuff about her, hoping for a fight, as she walked past in the corridor. She wasn't exactly well loved, by anyone. But I hadn't expected that they'd think she was dead. This was serious.

'It might not be that, though. There's no body, is there?'

'No, love. They're going to look, but nothing yet.' She tried to smile but she couldn't.

'Well then. Maybe it's not ... maybe she's OK then!'

Mum nodded, her mouth tightly shut. Janie started to cry and Mum went to get up.

'Don't, I'll get her,' I said. I was glad to get out of there. I lifted Janie out of her playpen. 'Wet nappy!' I called. 'I'll do it!'

I took Janie upstairs and set her down on the changing mat on the floor while I looked around for nappies. I was the only one who knew for sure that Nollaig was alive. I couldn't let people think she was dead, could I? Mum was gonna kill me when I told her, but it would be worse if I left it and she found out later. What was I meant to do? I'd promised Nollaig. She'd never speak to me again if I touted on her. Maybe there was some way to let people know that she was alive without them finding out where she was.

Janie waggled her fat little legs and gave me a toothy grin.

'Everything OK?' called Mum.

'Yeah, no problem. I'll keep her up here for a bit.'

'OK, love. I'll get the dinner on. Chips th'night.' She was managing to keep her voice steady.

'Great, Mum.' I lifted Janie. 'C'mon, Missus.'

I took her into my room and set her on the bed. Janie loves

my room. I think she likes the flower mural – all the pinks and purples. She bounced on the bed, stretching her chubby hands towards the flowers, as if she was trying to pick one of the roses. I built a wall of pillows around her so that she couldn't fall off the bed, and dug out a Disney DVD from the box under my bed. *The Little Mermaid*, her favourite and mine too. I stuck it on and she screamed in delight as the colours buzzed on the screen. I sat beside her and soon we were settled – Janie, surrounded by the pillows, rocking from side to side with the music, babbling in her funny toddler language, and me, sitting next to her and singing the words, trying to concentrate on this moment with her. How innocent she was, like a new bud, still closed and protected from the world. She didn't know anything other than how to be honest, and all I could think of was how to lie, what untruths I could dream up. If I could go back and be a baby and do it all again . . . but nobody can, can they?

I dug out my phone and sent a message:

To: NOLLAIG
Msg: Problem. Ppl think you're dead. We need a new plan. Mum freakin out.

A minute later and my phoned pinged, making Janie jump.

To: STEPHEN
Msg: She's not the only 1. Vicar came to see me today. School wants to have a memorial service!

Oh shit. What the hell were we going to do now?

22

Nollaig

People always ruin everything.

We'd had a great thing going. The mattress under the table that we'd made out of old curtains and an old foam chair pulled to pieces wasn't exactly comfortable but it wasn't far off, and the vicar, Brian, but it was hard to call him that somehow, had said he'd try to get a proper mattress. The room was warm because he'd brought me a heater, and I had candles now and stuff to read, even if it was the religious books that Stephen had predicted. They were OK, though, those books. One of them was by this guy who used to be in a really violent gang in New York. The first half of the book was all about his crappy childhood and how the gang made him feel like he had a proper family at last, but how they also got him into drugs and really bad fights with knives. He went to jail and that's where he met this preacher guy who told him all about Jesus and then his life changed and he didn't want to be a criminal any more. The book was pretty boring after that. Being good and having an ordinary life isn't much of a story, I suppose. But it was better than being afraid or being alone. I'd make sure things were as ordinary as possible for me and the baby.

The vicar had been bringing me food and leaving it underneath the angel, like we'd arranged. It was pretty nice food too; fresh sandwiches made with those French rolls, and pasta mixed up with tuna and sweetcorn. A lot nicer than anything I ever had at home. Sometimes he even left a flask with hot food in it – soup mostly and sometimes stew – and now that I wasn't feeling sick all the time I suddenly wanted to eat constantly, like I was making up for all those days when I couldn't keep anything down. If I hadn't been 100 per cent sure that the belly sticking over the top of my trousers had a baby inside I'd say it was the result of eating twice as much as I was used to. He was a pretty good cook. At home I used to make myself sandwiches a lot and sometimes those instant soup-in-a-cup things. I knew how to cook a bit – we did it in school – but I mostly couldn't be bothered. I never wanted to stay in the house longer than I had to.

Sometimes Dad went mental if there wasn't any food in the kitchen but he never ate it anyway, it was just an excuse to have a go. One time he made me cook stuff in the middle of the night. I'd gone down to the kitchen for a drink of water and got the fright of my life when I turned the light on and he was sitting there, upright at the kitchen table, his eyes staring madly straight ahead.

'Where's that bloody fish pie, Nollaig?'

'What bloody fish pie?'

'Don't you bloody swear at me, I'll knock yer block off.'

I rolled my eyes and went to walk out of the kitchen. He jumped up and grabbed my arm, jerking me back into the room.

'Ow! Let go!'

'Not till you've made that fish pie. It's good for you, fish.'

'You're pissed, Dad. Go to bed. Let me go – you're hurting me!' I tried to struggle out of his grip, but he tightened it.

'Ahhhhh!'

'Shurrup! C'mere.'

He dragged me over to the fridge.

'Now get the bloody fish and make it.'

But of course there was no 'bloody fish' in the bloody fridge. So he had me walk down to the twenty-four-hour garage and buy tins of tuna and sardines, and I was up till 3 a.m. making a stupid fish pie that nobody was going to eat. He sat the whole time, watching me with his mad eyes, and when I'd put it in the oven he made me sit at the table with him until it had cooked. We both sat there, saying nothing, and all I could think of was – where did my dad go – the real dad – the one I used to sit at this table with, eating breakfast cereal while I did my homework after school? I wondered if he was thinking it too. Or maybe a person can get so far away from themselves that they can't think of anything really. Anyway, the oven timer went off, I took the disgusting tuna and sardine pie out of the oven, and he stood up, shook my hand, and went to bed without a word.

I returned the flask to the vicar with a new note each time saying what I needed – loo roll, shampoo, more food. But he always left more than I'd asked for. He even left some of his old t-shirts, which I was really glad of because there was no way any of Stephen's skinny-fit band t-shirts were going to fit me.

I got to like the vicar, Brian I mean, even though we never spoke and I hadn't seen him since that day when we'd threatened him. Every day I checked the *What to Expect When You're Expecting* book for the food he'd left but he never left anything I couldn't have, and he even left a bunch of the stuff you were meant to eat – things with iron in, like Stephen had said. I guessed that he must have remembered what it was like when his wife was pregnant. But I tried not to think about her and his kids. I knew from the book that everything was basically OK and I skipped the pages that said I should be having hospital appointments and going to classes about giving birth. In fact I skipped everything about giving birth.

Sometimes I wondered about the world outside. What people were doing. What I was missing in school. School seemed so far away now. Coursework and teachers going on about GCSEs. It was stupid, but I missed it a bit – the everyday boring things that make life normal. But it wasn't just school, everything seemed far away. Sometimes Stephen brought the newspaper with him but I tried not to read it because it made everything seem weird; the world going on as it always does, and me hiding from it. And when I thought about things like that it made me remember that what I was doing wasn't really normal. That people having babies were meant to do things a different way. So I didn't read the papers, and I tried not to think about the world outside too much.

On Sundays I'd hole myself up in my little room, as promised, quiet as anything. Before people arrived I'd push the old sofa against the door in case anyone tried to get in. One week, one of the little kids, she must have been about five or six, started going, 'Miss! Miss! What's behind that door?' and the teacher said, 'Nothing, Molly, colour in your picture of the disciples.' But she was going on and on and then I heard a chair scraping back and her little fists on my door.

'Who's in there?' she sang. 'Who's there? Is it God and Jesus?' My heart was pounding. She must have been tiny and there was no way she could have shifted the door by herself, but it was weird being so close to being discovered like that. I sat on the sofa to make it extra heavy and closed my eyes and tried to focus on the Bible reading that the Sunday School teacher was giving. Eventually the little girl must have toddled off, but I sat there long after all the Sunday School noise had stopped, until I was extra sure that the church was empty. The baby was jiggling under my skin, unaware of anything. I like it here, I thought, as long as we're alone, or with Stephen.

It was feeling more and more like our place, like a kind of home. It was as if the people on Sundays were the ones who weren't meant to be here, not us. And then, everything changed.

He had come to see me during the day. I was listening to his CD again, but this time I heard him coming, because since that first time I'd learnt to listen to music with just one earphone on, the other can clamped to the side of my head, leaving one ear free to listen for unwelcome visitors. But although I could hear someone approaching there was nothing I could do, because I was in my room with no way out. I couldn't even drag the sofa across the door because it would have made a noise. Why hadn't I thought of a plan for this situation? Another way to hide?

When the door opened and I saw that it was him I was relieved. At least it wasn't someone else. But I was annoyed as well. I didn't want to see him.

'What do you want?' I scowled at him, taking off the headphones and clicking 'stop' on the CD player. The disc whirred as it spun to a standstill in the few seconds of silence.

'I brought your food . . . '

'Why didn't you leave it at the angel?'

'I need to talk to you, Nollaig. Can we have a chat, please?'

He looked serious. His face looked older than I had remembered and he didn't seem as fat as before. Same navy blue jeans but they sagged a bit around the top of his legs now. You could tell he was thinking the opposite about me as he stared at my belly.

'Seen enough?'

'Oh. Em, sorry.' He averted his gaze. 'Look, can we talk?'

I sighed. What harm could it do now?

'Fine. Can we have tea again?'

'Um. Yes, I suppose so. OK.'

I was gasping for a cup. The vicar frowned as he turned away from me. 'Come on then.' I followed him up the stairs to the main bit of the church. I could see that the snow had started again by the way the light was shining through the angel in a moving lace pattern. Mary's face was lit up too, as if the angel had caused it by flying in and zapping her with news from God. I hadn't heard any weird voices since the day I came to the church. It was just a window now.

'You like that window, don't you?' said the vicar. He managed a half smile but I could tell his heart wasn't in it. 'Just milk, no sugar if I remember correctly?'

'Oh, um, yeah. Thanks.'

'I like it too.'

'What?'

'The window. There's a legend about it. They say that the angel Gabriel protects the church and everyone who comes here.'

I sat at the front row again, same place as before. I wished that the angel was protecting me now. I reckoned I wouldn't be sitting here listening to Brian making tea if he was. I could hear him in the little room, clumsily moving around, clanking cups together and walking into stuff, probably piles of books on the floor. Once again the heating hummed into life. This time he wasn't whistling, though. He appeared from the little room, forehead wrinkled, with the two steaming mugs of tea.

'So,' he began quietly, sitting down, 'something has happened, Nollaig, and I don't know what to do about it, and I, well, you need to try and understand the position I'm in . . . it's very difficult . . .'

'What's happened?'

I tried sipping the tea but it was too hot. I pulled my sleeves down over my hands so I could wrap them around the mug. The vicar rubbed his eyes.

'Your school has been in touch—'

'What? Did you tell them I was here?' I was getting to my feet, ready to make a bolt for it. I considered chucking the tea at him before I left.

'Wait. Wait. Sit down. No, I didn't tell them anything.'

My heart was thumping. Had Stephen said something? I'd never forgive him . . .

'They don't know you're here, Nollaig.'

'Well, what did they phone for then?'

'They,' he sighed and stared into his tea, 'they want to have a service. Of prayer and . . . sort of a memorial thing . . . '

'Why? A memorial for who?'

'You.'

'What? But that's insane! I'm not dead. For God's sake, I've only been gone five minutes. What the . . . '

'It's been more than three weeks, Nollaig. You've been missing for almost a month. They think you might be dead.'

Dead? The word slammed into me like a train. Why would they think that? I was surprised they even cared that I was gone. I pressed my hands tightly around the cup and let the heat burn through my sleeves.

'You really should add the milk after,' I said.

'Excuse me?'

'After you've taken the bag out. Then add the milk. Cools it down better.'

'What? This is serious, Nollaig.' His eyes grew narrower.

'You're telling me! You're not the one who everyone thinks is dead!' My voice echoed around the cold building and I dropped it down to a loud whisper. 'You're not the one they're going to have a bloody service for. What the hell? Is my dad going to be there?'

'I don't know. And with all due respect, Nollaig, this puts me in quite a difficult position.'

'What do you mean? You can't tell them. You can't!'

I had started to shake and the tea was splashing out and burning my wrist. The vicar gently took my mug and leant over the back of the pew, setting it on the seat behind me.

'Look at me, Nollaig.' He looked directly into my eyes and spoke firmly. 'This has to stop now.' He took my hands in his. 'Please, listen. You are going to have a baby and neither you nor I are experts on babies. Anything could be happening in there.'

He looked at my belly and so did I. He was right but I didn't want to think about it. It was as bad as thinking about going home. I bit my mouth shut, trying not to cry. He continued. 'We need to get you to a safe place where you can be seen by a doctor and where you and your baby will be looked after.'

'Oh and that would suit you, wouldn't it?' I was trying to sound tough but I was crying now and it was coming out all pathetic. I wrenched my hands out of his. 'All you're worried about is your little secret getting found out, isn't it?'

'No.' He sighed and stretched back on the hard pew. He spoke slowly. 'I'm not going to pretend that I'm not worried about it, but I'd be in trouble for hiding you as well, and I don't think I can keep this up much longer, Nollaig.' He straightened up and looked at me but I didn't look back. 'It's just ... it's wrong. It's wrong of me to hide you here.'

'Yeah well,' I sniffed, staring straight ahead, 'it's wrong of you to have an affair too, isn't it?' But I knew that I didn't sound threatening.

'I'm not ...' he began. 'Look, it's not what you think. I only want what's best for you. How can I stand up there and lie to everyone?' He indicated the front of the church. 'How can I watch them all being sad about you, whenever I know you're only a few feet away? You have to trust me, Nollaig, it would be wrong to do this.'

I did trust him. In a weird way blackmailing someone is a bit like trusting them. He could pull the plug at any time – let everyone know everything – and now it looked like he might. But maybe he was right? Maybe this was all just going to get worse and worse, and maybe I should just give in. It was so exhausting. I grimaced as a pain jabbed into my side.

The vicar jumped. 'Are you OK?'

'Yeah. It was just a kick.'

'Are you sure?' He was sweating.

'Yeah! Happens all the time. She's dead wriggly.'

I couldn't help smiling. I loved it when she kicked me, even though it hurt sometimes. The vicar looked relieved. I knew then. It was like she'd kicked me awake to tell me that she was OK. That if I could get the vicar to keep his gob shut then every-thing would be OK.

'I'll tell you the truth,' I said to him, staring him in the face, 'I don't really care about you having an affair. Like, I think it's bad, but it's none of my business. And I don't like blackmailing you.' His eyes looked pleading. 'But I have no choice.'

He breathed out, hard.

'It's true. You don't understand. My dad . . . he's not a good person.'

There was a silence. He was listening. Waiting for me to say more.

'So anyway. I can't go back to him. That's never going to happen. I'll run away again. I'm not living with him, ever again. OK?'

'OK.'

'And I know you probably think I should just phone up social services or something. Well, I thought of that too. Do you know what they do to kids round our way who can't stay at home?'

'There's Fitzwilliam House.'

'Exactly.'

He knew about it. Everyone did.

'I'm so sorry, Nollaig. Things have been very difficult for you.'

'Yes,' I said, both hands on my belly, 'and I need to do what's best. For the baby. See, if I go back now they'll take her off me, and I can't risk that, because she's all I've got.'

He rubbed his eyes with both hands and frowned. He didn't have a better idea. He knew I was right.

'You probably have lots of friends,' I continued. 'Even if you lost your job, you could get another one somewhere, being a vicar somewhere else. I bet vicars have affairs all the time and then they just go and be vicars somewhere else.'

He was shaking his head, like I was a stupid kid and I didn't get it, but I didn't care.

'Either way. I can't let you tell on us. You have to do the service. Make it short or whatever. And don't worry – no one'll come anyway, I'm not exactly popular. But just do it and then they'll leave you alone, OK?'

I was talking to him like I was the adult, telling a child how things were going to be. It seemed mad considering I had no idea what I was doing. But I was thinking so clearly now. The baby inside me was getting herself ready to come out and she was going to be better than all of us – better than me, stealing money off Dad and nicking stuff from the shops, better than the vicar, now weakly rubbing his temples like he couldn't cope, better than Stephen, falling for a total idiot just because he paid him some attention. She'd be better than all of us because babies are pure and good, and she would need me and I would need her too. I was going to start it off right, and that meant protecting her right from now, even if it meant being stronger than adults.

'Sorry,' I said, getting up. 'Excuse me.'

He moved out of the pew to let me out, his head hung in defeat.

'Thanks for all the stuff, by the way.'

He looked up. 'No problem,' he whispered.

I walked down to my room and texted Stephen.

23

Stephen

'OK, so, I've found out what I could and I brought you these.' I handed the newspapers to Nollaig.

I had run from home to school that morning, willing the day to go more quickly, but of course it hadn't. The minutes and hours dragged by with hardly anyone mentioning Nollaig and I was only able to snatch a bit of gossip before Janet Parker and Carol Magee ducked into the girls' bogs. Mark was with them so I didn't want to get too close, I'd been trying to avoid him.

'I heard she jumped in the Lagan with no clothes on,' said Carol. The other two screwed up their faces in disgust.

'Jaysus. Why would anyone *do* that? It's dead selfish, isn't it?' replied Janet.

'Yeah well,' said Mark, 'she was always a bit weird.' He gave me a sly look out of the corner of his eye as he spoke.

Fuck him. Fuck them all.

When the final bell went I ran to the newsagents, grabbed all the local papers, and set off for the church, as fast as I could. I needed to talk about this and Nollaig was the only one I could talk to.

'What the hell are we going to do?' I said. 'Look at this!'

Page ten of the *Hope Street Gazette*:

A prayer service will be held for Nollaig Duffy in St Anthony's Church on Greymount Road at 12 p.m ...

'And it's been on the friggin' news now as well, Noll. I heard Carol Magee saying the *Sunday Life* had been on at her to do an interview.'

'Carol Magee? Uh, why? She hates me.'

'I know. I didn't hear the rest of what she said.'

'God,' Nollaig said, but she didn't seem that bothered. Didn't she understand?

'It's serious!' I said. 'What are we gonna do?'

She sighed and gave me a smile and came over to the sofa to sit beside me.

'Look, I know it's weird. But it's going to be OK. I've sorted it.'

'Wha? Has the vicar been leaving you some dodgy fags or something? In what universe have you *sorted it*?'

Her face dropped and she crossed her legs and turned away from me. She definitely looked serious now.

'At least I'm not going around panicking like a loser,' she muttered. 'At least I've tried to do something.'

'Look,' I said, calm as I could, breathing out as I spoke, 'sorry. Tell us how you've sorted it. This is serious, though. My mum's going nuts and I can't watch her crying and everything, and what if she wants to go to that service?'

Nollaig turned back to me but she still had her legs crossed, arms too, although that made me want to laugh because they didn't reach properly over her belly.

'I spoke to our vicar and persuaded him not to tell. He won't, OK? And you can't either. This is a glitch. And actually,' her eyes grew bright, 'it could work to our advantage.'

'Wha? How the feckin' hell could it work to our advantage?'

'Look, shut up talking to me like I'm thick, OK? It's not you that's stuck here with heartburn and a lumpy mattress.'

She was right, in a way. Whatever I had to face from Mum, she was in more trouble than I'd ever be. So full of plans all the time, but I wondered if she'd thought about how she was going to look after a baby all by herself. I fistled about in my bag and took out a pack of cinnamon rolls.

'Want one? They're pretty nice.'

'Ta.'

We sat there munching bread for a couple of minutes. I hadn't eaten since breakfast. I'd been hyper all lunchtime, trying to follow kids around for snippets of news.

'How could it work to our advantage then?' I said, mouth full.

'Well. It's not like I was planning to go away forever. If everyone starts thinking about me now and feeling bad about me having run away . . . '

'Or being dead . . . '

'Yeah, OK, or being dead . . . well, they might be glad to see me when I show up again. And I'll have a baby, won't I? So maybe they'll be nice to her too.'

'Her?'

'Yeah, I think she's a girl.' She smiled at her belly, rubbing it gently with both hands.

I wondered if she could be right. I mean people could hardly be angry with her for not being dead, could they? And as long as the vicar and me could keep it quiet for a bit longer ... But that was going to be the problem, wasn't it? Mum had been so upset last night. I'd never seen her so sad, not even when Rob was being his most evil.

'I still don't know about it, Nollaig. It's going to be very hard keeping this from Mum any longer.'

She shot me this panicked look and clutched the bump, like I'd been threatening to give her a kicking or something.

'Please, Stephen. Please.' Her face drained of colour. 'At least you've got a mum. I don't have anyone. I need my kid to have me.'

I hate seeing people cry. Especially people who are usually strong. I thought of all the times that Nollaig had come through for me. How she always let me come over, even when I'd been wrapped up in Mark for weeks. I'd text her when he stood me up or whatever, and she'd be over in ten minutes, or I'd go to hers if her da was keeping away. One time she brought round three massive bags of marshmallows. God knows where she got them.

'What are they for?' I asked her, my eyes red from the latest drama.

'Chubby Bunnies, you numpty!'

'Wha?'

And for the next hour she made us play Chubby Bunnies: stuffing marshmallows into our mouths to see who could get the most in. Both of us had tears streaming down our faces by the end of it. And now here she was, looking small and broken.

'OK. OK, I'll do it. Don't cry, Noll.'

What was I meant to do? Mum crying in the kitchen, her crying here? But she was right – she didn't have anyone else.

She cried harder when I spoke, and she reached out and grabbed my hand and said 'Thank you!' over and over. I knew it was the right thing to do then. Other people would get over our lies, and maybe, if we played it right, they wouldn't even realise we'd been lying. Either way, I had to help her. But now I was thinking about something else. Something I had to do, for me. Something I never thought I'd ever do in my life.

24

Stephen

I knocked on his door quietly at first. Maybe if he didn't hear then I wouldn't have to go through with it. I didn't want to talk to him. But I knew I had to.

I had left Nollaig, asleep on her side on the mattress. We'd spent the rest of the afternoon trying to distract ourselves by gossiping about school, reading the old magazines I'd brought from our house – rescued off the recycling pile. My mum likes those magazines that show you rich people's weddings and houses. They hardly have any stories in them, mostly pictures of expensive-looking people in their luxurious living rooms, draped over white leather sofas with their babies in designer gear. I look at them sometimes but they're mostly boring and you can tell they aren't wearing their own clothes because the magazines are always showing off the same designers' clothes. Anyway, Noll and I had a good laugh giving the posh celebs marks out of ten for hotness (Josh Hutcherson: Me: 7/10, not ideal as he'd be shorter than me, but I wouldn't turn him down. Noll: 2/10, Josh Hutcherson is not her thing at all. Johnny Depp: Me: 8/10, loses 2 points for dressing up as a pirate. Noll: 10/10, quite likes pirates) and then we thought about what we'd do if we had that amount of cash. Boring stuff, like houses, were disallowed. Me: have my own gallery showing all my own work and host celebrity parties once a month. Noll: custom made pirate ship. And so it went on.

And then I left and I went straight to his house and I stood outside it and forced myself to knock on the door.

It opened very quickly. He must have been standing in the hall. When he saw me he looked confused for a minute and then he suddenly clicked who I was and he nearly pissed himself. He stepped out onto the doorstep, gingerly glancing behind him.

'Wife in, is she?' I said. I knew it was evil of me but it was hard not to smirk.

'Shut up!' he whispered, scowling. 'What do you want?'

A voice came from inside the house.

'Who is it, Brian?'

I giggled to myself. Brian. Funny to think of him with a normal name and normal wife and everything. Wonder what she'd think if she knew about him? Poor cow.

'Uh, um, just someone from the church, dear, won't be a minute!' he called.

Good at lying, aren't you? I thought, as the vicar shut the door gently.

'What are you doing here?' he demanded.

'We need to talk.'

174

'What? We've nothing to talk about. Go away, please,' he hissed. 'Go away or I'll tell someone.'

'Yeah. It's about that. Sort of. We have to talk about Nollaig.'

'I don't want to. I—'

'Look, *Brian*,' I started, looking him up and down, like he was the last person I wanted to talk to, 'I don't exactly want to hang around with you either. But we both know this thing's gotten out of hand. We need to talk about it. So you're gonna meet me, in an hour, at the park. Bench at the side gate, beside the rose bushes, OK?'

I turned my back and walked off, leaving him gawping at me in silence. I knew he'd show up. An hour was just enough time. It would give him a chance to talk to his wife and make up some other lie about where he was going, and it would give me a chance to think about what the hell I was going to say to him.

Somehow, in the space of that next hour, I managed to think of a hundred and one things apart from the one problem I needed to solve. I helped Mum work out how to do her bank stuff over the computer, then I helped Janie eat her dinner (and we got most of it in her mouth), then I went upstairs and thought of a new Art project – a new collage using the petals of lots of different flowers all from the park. I knew I was meant to be thinking up a plan but Noll was the one who was good at that sort of stuff, not me. But still, there were things we could do to make it less bad, weren't there? Things that the vicar could say and not-say at that prayer service. I had to make sure we did our best.

He was sitting there in the half light, right where I'd told him to be. I still did a double-take, though. It was strange seeing him there instead of Mark. Mark, who hadn't spoken to me properly since the last time we sat on that very bench. My chest tightened at the thought of him. I hadn't been back to the park since then, I'd avoided taking Janie there, but it seemed like the right place to meet the vicar because it was the place of doom now. Besides, no one ever came to this end. Even in summer the only person you ever see is the gardener tending his roses.

I walked over to the bench. It was wet with melting snow and I scraped off what I could and sat down. The vicar said hello but he didn't smile. He was wearing this old bloke's mac that was tied tightly around his belly. Clueless. I said hello back.

'How did you know where I lived?' he asked.

'Saw you going in one day.'

'Oh.'

There was a pause. I knew I was going to have to start the conversation.

'So,' I said.

'So,' he repeated, sighing.

'So, about Nollaig,' I said, 'I think we need to talk about this whole "prayer service" thing. I've got some tips about what to say.'

He looked at me as if I'd just suggested firebombing the church.

'You cannot be serious. That girl is. At. Risk—'

'And you're at risk too, don't forget.'

He breathed in sharply and then there was silence.

'So, now that we've agreed that the best thing to do is to go ahead with the service,' I went on, 'I think we need to talk about what has to be said and not-said.'

'I don't understand what you mean,' he muttered.

'When you're talking, at the service, you have to play down the death thing. Because as soon as she's sixteen she plans on getting a council house and coming home. So just remember that – you don't want people to get all upset when they see her walking down the street like she's a big pregnant zombie or something. The baby will be a shock enough for most people. Oh, and that's another thing.'

He raised his eyebrows like he was wondering what on earth was next.

'She's going to have a baby, right? So you've got to go on about being nice to people and everything, because she's going to need some help when she comes back.'

'Being nice to people?'

'Yeah. Less of the "God will judge you" crap and more of the "do unto others" bit. Right?'

The vicar shook his head and dropped his tone.

'You've got me all wrong, Stephen,' he said, softly.

But I didn't think I had got him wrong. I was pretty sure I had him just right, and I wasn't about to let him scupper Nollaig's chances of getting a life for herself, or my chances of getting out of this mess without Mum totally freaking out. I thought of the bra hanging up in Nollaig's room, a splash of bright pink in that dull grey squat.

'Whatever. But you have to do this for Nollaig, OK? Just . . . just say good things about her.'

'What like? Why don't you tell me something about her, general things, what kind of a person she is? Apart from . . . ' His voice trailed off. I guessed he was thinking 'apart from a teenage slut who blackmails vicars' but I couldn't be bothered arguing. It was freezing now and I wanted to get this sorted and get home.

'She's funny, and kind, and she sticks up for people who get bullied. Don't give me that look. We don't make a habit of blackmailing people, you know.'

He looked dead ahead.

'OK,' he said, 'funny, kind, heroic . . . and I'll tell everyone to expect her home in a bit and do a sermon about single mothers and how wonderful they are.'

I ignored the sarcasm in his voice.

'Yep. That'll do. I'm off home now. See you around.'

He shook his head like I was unbelievable.

'Fine. Goodnight, Stephen.'

I sauntered out through the green gates, leaving him there on the bench. I felt taller, somehow, and my head buzzed with the energy of having been in charge of the situation. It was easy, I thought, I'd beaten the crap out of him without laying a finger on him. As I left the park and turned onto the pavement I glanced back through the railing to see the vicar on the bench, still sitting there with his hands in his pockets, staring at the roses, and I shrank again, back to my old size, and I thought about that picture of Craig McRoberts and his dad on the front page of the paper, grinning like winners, and I thought about Rob, and I walked home feeling awful.

Dear Lord,

Brian here.

I asked you for help and now things are worse. I know I'm not a good person, but I'm trying. I'm trying to help Nollaig. If it wasn't for that wretched boyfriend of hers ... Oh, that's not entirely fair, he's just a child himself. I know that Alison suspects something. The other day she asked me where all our bread was going. I had to lie and tell her that I'd been craving cheese sandwiches. 'You're not pregnant, are you, dear?' She thought that was terribly funny. I couldn't even fake a smile. She knows. She knows I'm hiding something. I haven't been myself lately at all. I've been so snappy with the children and I'm sure they've noticed the way I have to 'pop out' more often than usual so I can go and leave things for Nollaig.

I haven't even been able to ... well, you know ... Veronica ... lately. I can't bear to in the midst of all this ... Perhaps it's for the best. And yet I know that if I could just ... well, I know that I would feel better and maybe I'd be able to relax and think clearly. But no, I can't. The guilt is too much. I have been hiding a child away in my church, sneaking food from our home to keep her alive, lying to my wife even more than usual, and now I have to prepare a memorial service for someone who isn't only alive but who is pregnant! Doubly alive! Oh God, what am I supposed to do? I can't tell anyone because it has been going on for so long ... can I? It would mean telling everything. And now there is so much to tell that I would lose everything for sure. And yet if I don't tell I am sure I will lose my mind. Perhaps I already have.

I'm afraid to ask you for any more help, Lord. But I don't have anyone else to talk to. Please help.

Amen.

25

Nollaig

Not many people get to attend their own funeral. I mean, I knew it wasn't a funeral, not really, but all those people thought I was dead and so it was close enough. I supposed that without a body this was the closest thing I'd get to having an actual funeral. What if I *had* killed myself? But I didn't want to think about that. I touched my round, hard belly. Two bodies in one.

Obviously I wanted to see the service. Anyone would. Stephen had said I should stay hidden and I knew he was right. Imagine what would happen if someone had spotted me at my own funeral-type-thing. But I'd be careful. I'd sneak up to the balcony before the service and wait there for it to start. I'd been locked up in the church for weeks with no telly and only a bunch of books to read, and I was getting sick of stories about bad kids finding Jesus, and boring old blokes bleating on about the Bible.

Obviously there was no coffin but there was a small photo

frame on a table. I couldn't see it from the balcony but I assumed it held a photo of me. Beside the table there was a Christmas tree decorated with those wonky chains that kids make out of coloured paper. I wished it wasn't there. Nobody should have to see a Christmas tree at a funeral. Or a memorial, or whatever it was.

I was sitting at the back in the shadows, hugged up against the wall. I knew it was a risk but I couldn't resist a look, I wanted to see who would come. But when I saw them I wished that I hadn't bothered. Most of them were people I didn't know. Even the ones that I recognised were people who couldn't give a toss about me when they thought I was alive.

The church was brighter than usual and it was warm. The vicar had obviously been in earlier to turn on the heat and maybe to practise his lines. He was sitting to the side of the front bit of the church, waiting while the organ played off key. The gathered people were whispering to one another. I couldn't make out the expression on the vicar's face but I hoped he was holding himself together. I comforted myself with the thought that he was obviously good at lying. There was a bright display of delicate pink roses and purple irises at the front of the church. I guessed that that had been Stephen's idea. His favourite flowers; a secret message to me that things were going to be OK.

I started to well up. His plan was to keep out of his mum's way as much as possible until I turned up again. I knew I'd asked an enormous favour of him and I hoped his mum didn't hate us afterwards. She was sitting in the front row, beside Stephen, looking straight ahead, not chatting to him, or anyone. He was doing the same. She was one of the only people that I was glad to see and I knew that if everyone who didn't really care suddenly disappeared the church would be empty apart from her and Stephen. I wondered how she'd feel if she knew this was all a lie – that I was alive and well and watching her from the balcony? Would she still care? How far can you push a person before they disappear along with the ones who never cared in the first place? I made up my mind that I'd repay them some day and then I pushed the thought out of my head and tried to focus on the spectacle below.

There was a handful of kids from school. What the hell were they doing here? Probably only came for the after-service sandwiches or to get out of double Maths. Carol Magee? Seriously? I wasn't sure she'd ever even spoken to me. Snobby cow. I watched her tottering up the aisle and sitting down daintily on the edge of a pew. Wearing black? Probably just an excuse to show off her legs in that tight skirt. And I thought I could see the shiny snooker ball head of Mr Quinn the IT teacher. The week before I left he told me I was headed nowhere but the dole queue. I wondered if he was thinking about that now? It was sickening really, all these people who never liked me pretending that they did. Oh God, Munter Mark was there too! I willed Stephen to keep his eyes facing forward. It would kill him to see Mark there.

And then I saw him. A thought crashed into my head as I noticed the back of his waxy green jacket: services like this aren't for the dead person, they're for the ones who get left behind. So all those strangers were here for my dad. He was sitting two rows behind Stephen and his mum. You'd never know what my dad was thinking because he never speaks when he's sober, and when he's drunk he's often shouting this weird angry language that doesn't make sense. Even he was only here because he had to be, but a chill ran down my back to see him sitting there so still, like a dead body, and it made me want to run down the stairs and barricade myself in my room again. The feeling filled me up like a tidal wave and I clutched my belly, like the baby was the thing that would keep me here – keep me real and alive when I wanted to dissolve out of existence.

When I realised that the whole thing was for Dad, this big pretence, it made me want to vomit. As the vicar started to speak, asking everyone to stand for a prayer, I kept my arms wrapped around my bump, so that my baby couldn't hear a word of it. She would never hear him, would never even hear about him. Dad didn't deserve this turnout. It wouldn't even make him happy. He used to be happy, years ago. In the kitchen he'd move the table and get me to stand on his feet, and he'd put on the radio and dance me round the floor. But that was a long time ago, and now the thought of it was like a knife in my chest, because something happened to him – he switched off the radio and never danced again, and he made sure nobody else did too. I hated him for making me miss him, but even hating him wouldn't make him change. I swallowed the breaths that wanted to turn into tears. Look at all those people down there, imagining that they're sad. If they knew him like I did, they'd be happy that I got away, even if getting away meant I had really died. All of that sympathy belonged to me and my baby. But it was too late to think about that now. I didn't want to hear it after all; all the fake prayers and the vicar's lies. They were sitting there like puppets, facing the front, doing what they were told – sit, stand, sing, pray – with the vicar conducting them. Everything neat, everything in order. Even the angel on top of the Christmas tree standing perfectly straight. And my angel in the window, quiet and dark.

I didn't want to see them turn around when it was over, their pretend-miserable faces approaching my dad to shake his hand and ask if he needed anything. I knew that I was the biggest liar of them all but I felt like the only honest one. The organ was blaring out another tuneless song to God:

> *Change and decay in all around I see.*
> *Oh thou, who changest not, abide with me.*

As the hymn came to an end the vicar stood up to speak and I knew I had to get out of there. How can you hate somebody, like really hate them and wish they were dead, and love them at the same time? It's not possible, I thought, because the one I love isn't here. He died ages ago. I looked at the flowers on the little table.

I couldn't listen to any more of it. I snuck down the wooden stairs at the back of the church. I crept away quietly, following the stairs down and down to the crypt, and went back to what I'd been doing before: not existing.

26

Stephen

So, yeah, it was weird. Sitting there, front row seat, at your best mate-who-isn't-dead's remembrance prayer service. There was this picture of her at the front of the church on a table, all on its own, in one of those manky pine frames from the Pound Shop. Nollaig in her school uniform, aged about eleven, a little kid, scowling like mad because they'd obviously made her wear her tie properly. It was like a pathetic little shrine. Was that all he could come up with, that picture? It probably belonged to her mum. Her dad probably didn't have any recent pictures of her.

My roses and irises looked great, though. I was proud of that. The only colourful thing in this place, apart from the kids' Christmas decorations. I was glad it wasn't her real funeral. I made a mental note to plan a few things for the real thing, should it ever happen before mine. I also made a note to write down something about my funeral, because this was really horrible. Darkness can be nice at Christmas – it makes things feel cosy. But at a funeral, whatever time of the year, you need colour to balance out the darkness. Light, good music, people who are sad but who smile at one another. Not this; nobody talking, everyone so still, the most bloody awful organ music . . . I'd hate for people to be depressed by my funeral. Well, you know what I mean.

My mum kept dabbing her eyes and sniffing, trying to be brave. She'd left Janie with Julia, our next door neighbour. Julia is Polish and she loves Janie. Her kids are all adults now and she wishes Mum would let her babysit more, so she was delighted to have the chance to take Janie for the afternoon. 'Have more babies!' she tells my mum with a wink sometimes. 'Oh have another! I will take care of them!' Mum really likes her but there's no way she's having more kids. She keeps saying that the only man she'll ever trust again is me.

The thought made me wince as the organ ground out a hymn that sounded like it belonged in a primary school version of *Phantom of the Opera* or something. Everyone stood up except for the vicar who suddenly remembered to stand a few seconds later. He mimed the words of the hymn, rubbing his temples every so often as if he had a bad headache. He was clearly bricking it. I just hoped he'd be able to keep himself together and do the right thing.

When the hymn finished he walked, slowly, to the front of the church. His hands were balled into tight fists. He took a breath, raised his hands as if to embrace the gathered audience, spread his fingers, and spoke in a loud, clear voice:

'Members of the congregation. Let us join together in prayer on this solemn occasion.'

And that was that, he was off. Oh my God, it was actually pretty impressive! Mr Professional Vicar took over from the bumbling idiot that Nollaig and I knew. He didn't stumble over his words once throughout the whole service. If you'd never met him before you'd think he was some kind of super-hero vicar – *Clergy Man* – able to leap multiple pews in a single bound. Heh. Through all the sitting and standing and sitting-again, singing, praying, reading Bible verses, through it all he was calm, confident . . . amazing really. I don't know what I'd been worried about. When it came to the time for him to speak about Nollaig he talked about her like he'd known her personally for years, but without that fakeness you normally expect from vicars.

'Nollaig was a spirited soul, wasn't she? Her friends and family spoke about her with such fondness and in their stories and descriptions I got the impression of a girl who was full of opinions, full of life, and full of love.'

Fuck me. He was right. But who else knew this? Everyone else thought Noll was a no-hoper. I had told her to hide and not to watch the service, but I wished she could hear this. He went on:

'She'd always stick up for the ones who were getting picked on, the ones who other people ignored. She was a brave young woman and those who knew her knew that through hard times and dark days she never gave up hope.'

My mum was blowing her nose loudly and truth be told I could feel myself getting emotional as well. He went on a bit about hopeful people being the ones to change the world, and that's when he said it – the shot to the heart – the thing that Noll and I needed him to say:

'And, people gathered here today, you must put your faith in hope as well. You must learn from Nollaig. You must never give up hope, for we know not where hope will take us.'

I could see my mum's face light up when he said it and I knew that it had worked. It was like someone had switched a light on in the place. The organ sang out, a faster tune than before, and everyone sprang to their feet and you could *feel* the lightness in their voices. This time the vicar wasn't miming, he was singing, loudly, and tapping his feet and beaming. He knew he'd done a great job and suddenly I could almost see the point of it all – everything he'd said had been kind of a lie, and kind of the truth – Nollaig was just a few feet away, not dead, but he'd been right about her – she was good, and hopeful, and somehow he'd made everyone love her properly, just in that moment, probably for the first time ever. I glanced behind me at their faces, full of joy: loads of them were crying and some of the kids from school were holding hands. It was like a proper miracle. All these fake, false people who'd come for who-knows-what reason were suddenly joined together and really being real.

I scanned the room, the faces from school, the teachers, a couple of people I didn't recognise, all singing, and Mark. Mark, standing with his head lowered. Maybe he felt me staring at him because he lifted his head and looked straight at me. My heart hammered against my ribs and I held his gaze for long enough to let my body feel the full impact of what I had lost. He lowered his head again and I wanted to throw up. I gripped my arm hard to remind myself of what was real – me, Nollaig, all these people finally getting it, finally understanding what they missed when she was alive, and I was the only one who still had her. That was more than any of them had. I dug my nails in hard. I'd feel something else, I was determined. Focus. Focus on Nollaig, on this day. Look around, who else is here?

Then I saw her dad. He was sitting in his pew with his head in his hands, sitting really still. I guessed that it was too much for him, the auld sod. He was a mean bastard, I knew it, I knew more than most people, because of what Nollaig told me, because of what I heard with my own ears: slut; bitch; hoor. But for the first time in my life I was looking at him and seeing him as just a sad, old, empty man. Bloody hell, Nollaig, I thought, you're meant to be missing or dead, gone forever, and you've somehow got me feeling sorry for your da.

When the service was over I slipped away, telling Mum that I was nipping to the loo and that I'd see her back at home, later. As everyone lined up to shake the vicar's hand I quietly made my way downstairs, hoping that Nollaig was well hidden, imagining the faces of the kids from school if they'd seen her at her own memorial service. I couldn't wait to tell her everything. She was hidden all right. But I hadn't been prepared for the state she was in.

27

Nollaig

I started getting *really* worried when I saw Stephen's face.

'Oh my God, are you OK? What's wrong?' he said, rushing over to put an arm around me.

I was on the sofa in my room when he came in and I couldn't look up at first. The pain. It was like someone had kicked me in the guts and it spread out across my belly and round my back. One of those moments where you forget to be scared because your brain is dealing with something really new – a pain that has come out of nowhere – not one that you could avoid by leaving the house, or by ducking at the appropriate moment. You couldn't be prepared for this kind of thing. As it subsided I was able to straighten up, and that's when I started getting worried.

'I don't know, Stephen! I don't know what's wrong. It's the baby. What am I going to do? There must be something wrong with the baby. Oh Jesus. What can I do?'

'I don't know!' he said.

And there we were, the two of us who always had a plan, and we didn't have a clue. I could feel the panic like an elastic band tightening around my chest, making it hard to breathe. Breathe. That's a start. Breathe, Nollaig. There is no pain now. Maybe it has gone and it was just one of those things. A pregnancy thing. Something you haven't read about yet.

'Get my book!' I pointed towards the fat book lying at the end of the table and Stephen grabbed it and started thumbing through the pages.

'Good idea. Where's the index? P, for pain . . . '

I wanted to look for myself but I let him do it. He had tears in his eyes. I knew he was thinking the same thing I was. If this was it, if something was wrong with the baby, was it our fault? For deceiving everybody? Is this what you get for lying to everyone and blackmailing people? I put my hands on my belly.

'She kicked! She kicked! It's OK, she's alive!'

Stephen looked up briefly and kept searching through the book.

Thank God. I put both my hands on my bump and silently told her to move again, but nothing happened. Maybe the scariest thing was that things just happen and we can't control them at all. I stared at Stephen, willing him to find the right information – the information that would tell me everything was OK. I was about to ask him to give me the book when he spoke.

'Listen to this, Noll: "Premature labour. You're in premature labour if you start to have contractions that efface or dilate your cervix before thirty-seven weeks of pregnancy. Call your doctor or midwife right away if you're having any of the following symptoms in your second or third trimester (before thirty-seven weeks): An increase in vaginal discharge; Vaginal spotting or bleeding; Abdominal pain, menstrual-like cramping; An increase in pressure in the pelvic area; Low back pain."'

'What does "efface" mean?' I said.

He shrugged. 'No idea. But have you got any of those other things? The bleeding or whatever?'

'Just the pain, I think.'

He wrinkled up his face and his lips moved as he read the piece again in silence. Then he closed the book and set it on the floor. I knew what he was going to say. And I knew he was right, but I didn't want him to be right.

'It says you should phone a doctor if you have any of them.'

'I know. But it was only one. Maybe it was a fluke. It might not happen again.'

He squeezed my hand.

'I'm fucking scared, Nollaig. We're in deep shit already and if something happens to you . . . '

'Oh, what? You're thinking about yourself? What about my baby? You don't think I'm scared too? You have no idea . . . I'm not going back to him . . . I'm not . . . '

But I was too scared to be really angry with Stephen. I closed my eyes and held my stomach, wishing that everything was OK. He didn't say anything else. He put his arm around me. That was when I noticed that we weren't the only ones in the room.

Dear Lord,

It is done. I have said my final words to my congregation.
I am going to find Nollaig now and I am going to end this
charade. It is time for the truth. The whole truth.

Even if I have nothing left after this day ends.

I hope that you at least will still be here.

Amen.

28

Stephen

I hadn't heard him opening the door. I jumped up and checked that there wasn't anyone behind us – that he hadn't brought Nollaig's dad down here or anything – but there was nobody, just him. We stood facing one another for a moment before he spoke again.

'Can I come in? I'd really like a word.'

I looked at Nollaig and she nodded. The vicar was in his normal clothes again. He came in and leant his bum against the table top to face us. I sat down but stood up again, I wanted to be at eye level with him.

'It was a good service. Thanks,' I said without smiling.

Well, it had been a good service, and much as I hated churches I had to be grateful that he hadn't cocked it up.

'What do you want?' said Nollaig, still clutching her bump. 'If you want us to say that we won't tell on you, then that's OK, we won't say anything. It's over now and we can go back to the way things were – you leaving food and whatever. OK?'

'No. It's not OK.'

'What?' Nollaig and I spoke in unison and he held up his hands like he was surrendering or offering peace.

'Nollaig,' he spoke her name warmly and looked at her, ignoring me, 'those people. Your friends, they—'

'I don't have any friends. And no family. I only have Stephen.' Her face was dark with anger.

'What about Stephen's mum? She clearly cares about you. And some of those people from your school?'

'They don't give a shit,' she spat out, but you could tell the vicar had got to her with that crack about Mum. She wiped at her eyes.

'Go away!' she yelled at him. 'Get lost. I don't want to talk to you.'

'You heard her,' I started. 'You should go.'

'Wait. Please, just wait,' said the vicar. 'I heard you talking. I was listening. You need a doctor. Please, for the baby's sake—'

'Get OUT!' Nollaig screamed, both hands in her hair – and suddenly she was bent double again.

'Nollaig!'

Her face was as white as his stiff collar and she had her eyes closed.

'Nollaig?' he shouted, shaking her arm. 'Nollaig, can you hear me?'

He turned to me, his eyes wide.

'Stephen. Pull her sleeping bag out and lay it on the floor.

Now!' He held her steady on the sofa as I dragged her stuff out from under the table.

I thought, what would I be doing if he'd left five minutes ago? No time to think about it now. He was lifting her onto the mat and telling me to help him. He laid her on her side and propped her leg out so she didn't fall over.

'She's breathing and her pulse is fine, if a little fast,' he said, with his fingers wrapped around her wrist. 'She's probably only fainted.'

I was sitting at her feet, motionless. I didn't know what to do so I draped one of the other blankets over her legs.

'Good idea, pull it up there,' the vicar said, and I did what I was told. To be honest I felt like I was in a trance. All I could think of was Nollaig. He was helping her. He knew what to do and I was glad that he was here because I was lost and my brain was telling me nothing. When he was finished checking her, Noll's eyes began to open. She looked confused for a minute and then she tried to sit up, but the vicar put a hand to her shoulder.

'Sssssh. Just rest, Nollaig,' he whispered. 'Stay there. You're OK, you just had a fright. Everything will be OK. Just rest.'

It was like she was in a trance too. She just did what he said. Closed her eyes again. I grabbed a pillow for her head and handed it to the vicar. As he lifted her head carefully and placed it under her he began to speak to me in the same tone of voice he'd been using for her.

'Stephen. I know you hate me.' He looked at me, frowning, beads of sweat beginning to appear on his forehead. 'I know you think I'm a bad person. But I know you love Nollaig as well.'

I knew what was coming and I didn't know how I was going

to respond. A bomb had gone off in my brain and suddenly it was chaos in there – so many different voices telling me what was best, and the loudest one sounded like Nollaig's but she wasn't making any sense because she was telling me to give in and not give in – to get the doctor and not to send her home – to save her baby from harm and to save her baby from being taken away. I didn't know which voice to pick. Everything seemed like a bad idea. I couldn't take it. My body started to tighten up. Why did everything have to be on me? It was her decision to run off, her responsibility, she was the one who got herself pregnant ... and as the thoughts were piling into my brain I felt myself running as well, out of the room, across the children's playroom, up the stairs.

I could vaguely hear the vicar calling after me but his voice seemed distant compared to the ones yelling in my head. At the top of the stairs I began running towards the altar. I wanted to kick over the lectern and rip up the stupid hymn books and bash my fists across the keyboard of the electric organ. I brushed past the Christmas tree and caught sight of its coloured paperchains. I shoved the tree out of my way and it made a light crunch as it fell to the floor beside the little table with Nollaig's picture. There was a door open – a door to the graveyard outside – I could feel the icy breeze drawing me out of the wide, dark church, and I ran towards it because I wanted to be out of there, away from this place, away from this decision and the voices and the vicar and ...

'Stephen.'

I heard my name. Clearly, as if someone was standing beside me. I stopped and turned right around, but there was nobody there. The sunshine was pouring through the stained glass window and the angel's face was glowing. But in the corner of the window sat Mary on her knees, in the shadows. I couldn't take my eyes off her. The angel towered above her like maybe it was going to kill her, but the look on her face, it wasn't a look of fear, it was a look of determination, and her eyes were gazing at the face of the angel. I remembered that I had called the vicar a coward. That made two of us then. And I knew I couldn't leave Nollaig because she'd been there for me when I needed her. I'd be by her side in that hospital. I'd be there if they tried to take her baby away, I wouldn't let them. I turned around again, shut the door to the outside, and walked back towards the crypt.

29

Nollaig

I could hear them whispering and I wasn't sure if I was dreaming or not until I opened my eyes and everything was as clear as it had been before. Before the pain. I remembered now. The vicar and Stephen, arguing. I had been thinking about what to do and wondering if maybe, having come so far, this really was the end of it all. And then, the pain had come. It came like before – a stab to the guts that spread all the way around to my back. But it was worse this time. It took my breath away so that I couldn't cry out. Everything went white. And when I woke up things had changed; everybody was taller. No, I was on the floor. And they were talking about me. I could hear them saying words that made me feel safe and scared all at the same time. Ambulance. Doctor. Baby. And then they were looking at me, and Stephen was coming over. He smiled and knelt down on the floor next to me.

'Hiya, Nollaig. We're going to phone the ambulance now, OK? Don't be scared about it. I'm going to make sure that you and the baby are OK.'

I was so tired that I gave in to believing him. I lifted myself up, resting my elbows on the pillow and then using my hands to sit up straight. Deep down I knew that his promise could hardly be true, but I had no choice but to believe him. They wanted me to stay lying down but I didn't feel like lying down. The vicar began to quiz me.

'How do you feel, Nollaig?'

'Um, OK, I suppose. Bit tired.'

'OK, that's good. Not sick or anything? Do you think you're losing blood?'

'I don't think so. No, I don't feel sick.'

'Good, good. Is your heart racing or anything like that?'

'No.'

He smiled. And then frowned, as if he'd just remembered something.

'And the baby, Nollaig. Do you feel any movements?'

I did. She'd been kicking the crap out of me since I'd woken up. Each little thump a reminder that I was two people. Little welcome jabs asserting her authority. I knew she was coming soon and that she'd fight her way out and that she'd be the only person in the world that I never wanted to run away from. I nodded and the vicar looked relieved.

Stephen helped me steady myself against the musty fabric of the sofa. The blood ran from my head and I felt a brief rush of dizziness. But the pain was gone and the baby was moving. We were OK, for now. I rested my face against the worn material.

When he was sure I was comfortable Stephen got up again to face the vicar and I listened to them, one eye closed and one watching their uneasy conversation.

'They're on their way,' the vicar said, putting his phone back into his pocket. 'They said they might be half an hour or so.'

'Half an hour? That's forever! Anything could—'

'Ssssh!' The vicar glanced over at me. 'You'll frighten her. They're very busy – they have a couple of car accidents to attend to and they'll be here as soon as they can.'

'I can actually hear you, you know,' I said. But they ignored me and glared at one another.

'Nollaig's OK,' the vicar continued. 'She's conscious and talking and the baby's moving. She'll be OK but we don't know what the pain is. It might mean the baby's coming and—'

'It's too early!' I cried, suddenly more alert.

Stephen glared at the vicar. 'Now who's scaring her?'

'Sorry.' The vicar looked down at his feet and then towards me. 'I didn't mean to scare you, Nollaig. It is too early, but doctors can do amazing things and lots of babies come prematurely. My own girl was premature.' He paused and took a breath. 'You'll be OK. They're on their way. Try to keep calm.'

But I couldn't keep calm. Too early didn't just mean too early for the baby to be born. It meant too early for me, because I wasn't sixteen yet. This is what Stephen had meant about keeping me safe! Oh God. They were going to take her away, I knew it! I wished that I could cry but no sound would come out and no tears would come.

Stephen had his arm around me and he was looking at the vicar as if he was the devil.

'I think you should shut up now. You've scared the shit out of her.'

I didn't like his tone. I looked at his hands. You know Stephen's going to snap when he starts flexing his hands. My heart was racing. The vicar was getting into a state and Stephen was eyeballing him. I didn't want this. A storm was brewing in the hot silence between them.

Then the vicar's eyes briefly turned towards me and he dropped his gaze to the ground and sat down on a chair. The air seemed to cool. He folded his arms.

'Nollaig. I apologise. Everything will be fine for you. As for you,' he turned to Stephen, 'I won't allow you to make me angry any more. We must concentrate on Nollaig now.'

I felt my face relax.

We sat in silence for a while and I could feel the heat of Stephen's face against mine. I knew he was boiling as he gripped me tightly. I wanted to hear something. I wanted there to be words. Anything instead of the things I was thinking about the baby being born too early, about her being taken away, about the pain returning, about the ambulance being too late . . .

'Stephen,' I said, my eyes half open.

'Yeah?'

'Tell me about something.'

'Wha?'

'Anything. Tell me something.'

'Like what?'

'I don't know. Something I haven't heard before. Tell me about why you hate religion so much.'

'You probably know why already.'

'I don't. Not really.'

Stephen scowled. The hand that gripped my shoulder was clammy. But I wanted to hear it now. It was something other, something to get my head into that was nothing to do with babies and hospitals.

'Tell me. Please.'

'OK,' he said, eyeing the vicar, 'I will.'

30

Stephen

The day my mum came home and told me she'd met a bloke in church I was dead happy. It'd been just us two for ages and, truth be told, you could tell she was feeling the strain a bit. I'd stopped going to church a couple of years since but I hadn't had a problem with her going really. It was all made-up stories as far as I was concerned. Pretty harmless. But I didn't like the way that they sometimes looked down on people. Like one time the vicar did this sermon about why everything had gone wrong in the world and it was all about Adam and Eve and the Garden of Eden, and Eve eating the apple and then, BOOM, it all fell apart, and now everything crap could go back to that point and we could blame those two for mucking it all up.

Rubbish story anyway, but the worst bit was when he started listing everything that was wrong with the world. Murderers (fair enough, most people thought murderers were bad), liars (them too. Who likes a liar?). But then he went on, his beady eyes glancing round the half-empty pews: 'Murderers, liars, fornicators, single parents, homosexuals . . .' I swear he looked right at my mum as he said 'single parents'. I asked her about it later as she was peeling spuds. I said I didn't think it was very fair. She put down the peeler and turned around to speak to me, like this was something dead important. She said that sometimes you just have to ignore stuff if you want to get on in life, and that not all battles were worth fighting.

She sounded so knackered when she said that, like she'd been ignoring stuff for a long time, so I didn't push her on it, and I didn't mention the 'homosexuals' either, because she had enough on her plate, but I didn't like it. And I didn't want to ignore it. I didn't think their story was any use anyway – how is it Adam and Eve's fault if some bloke goes out and murders someone in the twenty-first century? So I stopped going to church and my mum didn't mind and that was that. I was glad that she still went because some of the people there were pretty nice. They weren't too nosey and they did things like organising coffee mornings, and everything was going OK – she was meeting people, making friends. And then she met him.

He was the church warden, which meant he was in charge of the keys and the cleaning rota and stuff like that. Not a big deal but the way he went around you'd think he was the friggin' archbishop. The first time she brought him home he'd seemed all right but bloody hell was he boring, going on and on about church business over our Sunday roast. Every spoonful of peas he paused to tell me something else about why he was so crucial to the running of the church.

'Not everyone can have the keys, you know. It's a major responsibility having the keys. The last warden lost them, you know, and he only lasted two weeks after that. I keep them in my pocket and check them regularly throughout the day.' He patted his pocket so I could hear them jangle. 'Lose these keys, and I could lose my position!'

Boring auld git. But Mum liked him and so I made an effort, because she seemed happier than ever before, and I only had to put up with him on Sunday afternoons.

I don't know when it started exactly, all the heavy God stuff, but it was pretty soon after that. The vicar had put him in charge of opening up and locking up after a special prayer meeting. The meeting was called something like 'The problem of Sodom and Gomorrah in today's world' and they'd had a special speaker. The following Sunday I had to hear all about it. Mum and I sat in silence, scraping our knives and forks across the plate, picking at the roast chicken that I'd prepared.

'Dreadful thing this AIDS. You'd think it would have put them off, but no. There are more homosexuals now than ever before.' He took a big forkful of potatoes and stuffed it in his fat gob and he never stopped talking while he was chewing away. 'Spreading their disease all over the world, even here in Belfast! Imagine that! And they think that there are even teachers in our schools who are homosexuals – teaching our youngsters about their disgusting lifestyles. Bloody pansies. Praise the Lord that there is a cure, eh?'

My mum raised her eyebrows. 'A cure?'

'Yes, praise Jesus! There's special classes they can go to – coun-selling – to get it out of them.'

I tried to focus on my broccoli. I wished that he would shut up but he was so excited by the subject, or maybe just by the sound of his own voice.

'Yes, yes, these queers, they can get special prayers said, to put them out of the way of it.'

'That sounds quite extreme,' said Mum, quietly.

There was silence. I looked up at him and his face was stony. He was staring at Mum and I began to feel sorry for her, wondering what I could say to help, or maybe saying nothing was the thing to do, let it pass, like she'd said before. It was too late, though.

'Extreme?' He said the word like it was poison. 'I'll tell you what's extreme. Extreme is, is, these *perverts* going around converting children to their wickedness!' He stuffed in another forkful of potato. 'Extreme is them popping up on the television every five minutes, trying to make us all think that it's normal to behave that way! Extreme? Let me bump into one of them someday, I'll show them extreme!'

Mum went back to poking her chicken around on the plate. I assumed that this was one of the battles she'd decided couldn't be won. She was probably right because 'queers' and their filthy lifestyles became one of Rob's favourite topics of conversation, and the prayer meeting, as it happened, wasn't a one-off. It became a weekly thing with different speakers invited to talk about different aspects of the perversions of homosexuality. And lucky old us, we got to hear all about it every Sunday lunchtime.

But that wasn't the worst of it. Him going on and on about 'queers' all the time. That was just words after all, and when you're the gay kid in your class you get used to putting up with words. 'Oh my God, you're so gay.' That was me. *So gay*. I got into fights sometimes but I was clever about it. I'd find an excuse to beat the crap out of one of those kids that called me gay, but the excuse was always something different. I'd wait until they crossed me in another way. 'He just went mental, Sir. All I did was spill paint over part of his picture. It was an accident and it wasn't even a lot of paint! Psycho!' But I knew why I'd done it really. Not so 'gay' now, am I? I'd be thinking to myself as I pounded them to the ground. Broke a kid's nose once. He deserved it but I got suspended for a week and they told my mum that next time I'd get expelled. So I got good at reining it in – holding back – tuning them out. And I could tune Rob out too. Instead of finding him boring I started finding him hateful, but I kept it in, because when he wasn't banging on like Hitler about poofs and AIDS he was making Mum happy, bringing her flowers and telling her she was 'a great woman'. I have no idea how she fell for it but she did, and she obviously loved him, so I kept myself quiet when he started going on, and I tried to put all my energy into Art.

But then Rob moved into our house. I suppose he managed to miss all the church sermons about 'living in sin'. Or maybe he just made up his own rules, like they all do. Anyway, he invaded our house, and after that his bullying started going beyond just words.

The first time that he hit me it was just a light slap. We were at breakfast on a Saturday morning – him at the table getting served by my Mum as usual, me helping myself to cereal at the counter, my back to him as he gave off to Mum about his eggs being overdone. Then he started on me.

'And what are you up to today, Stephen? More of that poncy painting, I expect?'

I didn't turn around and didn't answer, just shrugged.

'Cat got your tongue has it? I asked you a question.'

I heard Mum clanking the dishes into the sink. Why didn't she ever say anything? Maybe she was just trying to keep the peace – waiting for him to calm down or go onto something else. I turned around to face him. Fuck me, he was ugly. Big red face, dripping egg all over his dressing gown. What the hell did she see in him?

'Yes. More of the poncy painting,' I said, deadpan. I turned back to my cereal, adding milk, looking for a spoon. He went on, talking with his mouth full.

'Time we got you down to church, lad. You'll come with me tomorrow. The devil makes work for idle hands.'

'Can't. I've got homework to do.'

'You'll come with me.'

I took a breath and turned around to look at him. I had to be careful. He was a lot bigger than me, and it could ruin everything for Mum, but at the same time I wasn't going to set foot in that place, not ever.

'No,' I said, 'I won't.'

And that was when he did it. He got out of his seat, casually walked over to me, and slapped my face. My mum gasped and dropped a knife, the margarine smeared the lino. I just stood there. I couldn't believe he'd done it. I wanted to kill him. I gripped the counter behind me and glared at him. He turned and walked off, without a word.

That was the start of everything. Our house became silent and cold, like the *Titanic* moving slowly towards the glacier. The only sound was the storm of Rob, ranting at Sunday lunchtime and giving me the occasional slap when he felt I'd been out of line. Once he punched me on the side of my head for staying out late. 'Spare the rod and spoil the child,' I heard him tell my ma one day. 'He needs knocking into shape that one. Godless wee . . . he'll be taking drugs and all sorts before you know it.'

But I never went to church with him. It became the way that I had power over him. He was getting Mum to go to church, even when she didn't feel like it, and she had to start dressing like an old lady in a long skirt and hat, because he made her. He was making her say grace at mealtimes to thank God for things like traditional families and the Queen. And every Sunday we had to hear about the Save the Gays prayer meeting and how many people they were praying for and how many conversions they'd made this week. Rob was put in charge of a team that went round the doors delivering leaflets that said things like 'Adam and Eve, not Adam and Steve! If you struggle with Same Sex Attraction Addiction please come to our meeting and find out how to break the curse.' I asked Mum about it one night when he went out with his leaflets.

'Why do you put up with it?'

She was drying the dishes, looking at the soapy water intently. She'd changed. She used to go out with her mates, have a laugh, come home half-pissed sometimes. She never saw them now. And somehow she didn't seem happy at all any more, but she still made his tea, still kept quiet.

She sniffed. 'He's not a bad man, Stephen. He provides for us, after all.'

'You used to do that. You don't even go to work any more.'

'Well, maybe we're lucky that I don't have to.'

But she wasn't looking at me and I knew she wasn't feeling lucky. I picked up a cloth and started helping her dry.

'Kick him out. We don't need him.'

She put down her cloth and closed her eyes for a second, before taking my arm and giving me a smile.

'Things are OK, Stephen. He's OK, really. I won't . . . I won't let him do anything . . . anything really bad. He said we'll get married soon. To make everything proper.'

'You're mad! Don't marry him, Mum! You're scared of him,' I said.

She gave me a look that said 'enough now' and then she changed the subject, asked me about school, and I knew it was my cue to leave it.

The funny thing was that it was school that changed everything. It was a Monday evening. We were sitting in the living room listening to classical music on the radio (because we weren't allowed the telly on when Rob was in – too many queers on the telly). I knew it was school when the phone went. I wished that I'd had the foresight to have taken myself off out for the evening. He hoisted his enormous bulk out of the armchair and crossed the room muttering to himself about people phoning at inconvenient times and with each ring my heart was pounding. He was going to kill me.

'Yes?' He answered the phone gruffly and I was glad. Maybe if they could pick up on what a nasty piece of work he was then they'd break it to him gently. He turned around to look at me. 'This is the man of the house. What's he done?'

I squirmed in my chair.

'Jesus, Stephen, what did you do?' Mum whispered.

I just shrugged. She'd find out soon enough. Rob's piggy eyes widened. His face went purple. He was nodding but making no sound. Then finally, 'Thank you,' he said, steadily, 'I will deal with this and you can rest assured that it will never, ever, happen again.'

He hung up, walked calmly over to the radio and switched it off. It gave me a minute to think. Should I say something? Should I quickly tell my side of things to Mum? Should I try to apologise, or should I face him out? I tried sizing him up. Could I take him? I didn't know, especially with the mood he was in, he'd be like a bull coming at me . . . and then I didn't have time to think any more because he was crossing the room and as he passed the fireplace he lifted a poker from the fire set and Mum screamed, 'No, Rob! Oh Jesus! Don't!' and he swung it out and brought it down on my shoulder, hard, as I sat on the sofa. Mum was screaming, 'Christ almighty! Oh Jesus Christ! Stop it, Rob!' and he growled as he turned to her, the poker still raised:

'Do you know what this is?' He looked at Mum as he pointed at me with the poker. 'This, this, little piece of filth? He's a queer!'

On the word 'queer' he brought the poker down again but this time I moved and it only caught me on the side. It gave me time to get up but when I tried to move the pain in my shoulder tore into me and I crumpled to the floor. He was ranting on and on as Mum cried and shouted at him to stop it.

'I told you! I told you what would happen if he wasn't

disciplined! Kissing some fella in the boys' toilets he was! Disgusting little shit.'

He dropped the poker and grabbed me by the collar of my shirt, bringing my face right up close to him. His breath was hot and sour. My head was buzzing with the pain and I felt like I was going to throw up.

'Deny it, you wee shite. Say you didn't do it.'

But I couldn't deny it, and I didn't want to. He was going to kill me and I didn't even care any more. Fuck him. Fuck them all – the God-fearing good people of the church and their club for bigots. He could beat the shit out of me but he wasn't going to beat who I was.

'No.' I could hardly speak. It was painful to move, to breathe. 'I won't deny it. I am a queer. I'm a big fucking faggot, and I love it, and I'm a better person than you'll ever be,' and I spat in his face, and I knew he was going to break every bone in my body and that it would be worth it because I'd have that image forever, his face when I said 'faggot' and the big gob of spit running down his cheek.

He started pounding me with his fist, holding me down, as if he needed to, with one hand, and punching me in the face and the stomach with the other.

And then, there was a loud crack. And it stopped. And Rob was lying on the ground beside me, dazed. And my mum was standing behind him looking wild like a banshee, holding the bottom of a heavy ceramic vase that she'd just broken over his head. She took three deep breaths and the voice that came out of her was more like a cry than words, but it said something urgent, something about getting out, and somehow we managed it, the two us, her shaking and me limping and coughing up blood, and we crossed the road to Mrs Kinnead's house and in a haze, right before I passed out in her hall, I heard Mrs Kinnead swear and tell my mother that everything would be all right.

31

Nollaig

'Holy shit, Stephen!' I said, wide awake now. The vicar and I were staring open mouthed at Stephen who was sitting in the same position he'd been in before, legs drawn up, hands clasped.

'And was it? Was it OK?' I asked.

Stephen shrugged. 'Still alive, aren't I?'

God. All the times I'd complained about my dad ... 'Why didn't you say anything before?'

'It's in the past, Noll. Me and Mum have Janie now. Everything's different.' He smiled at me.

'So that's why you hate religion?' the vicar said.

We both looked at him. He'd been so quiet. I was waiting for him to speak, to say something like 'We're not all like that!' but he turned his face away from our gaze.

'Yeah, that's why,' said Stephen. 'My mum even went to our

church to see what her vicar would do to help us, but he didn't want to know.'

'That's awful ... it really is ...' the vicar started.

'Yeah well. Rob had gotten there first, got his side in.' Stephen rolled his eyes. 'We moved after that, and we kept well away from churches.'

The vicar shifted his position on the table and undid his top button. 'I'm so sorry you had that experience.'

Nobody spoke or moved for ages. Stephen was still hugging his knees and I wondered what he was thinking. I wondered what time it was. I felt the baby wriggle and I wanted to laugh and tell everyone, but it wouldn't have been right. It was so quiet and still. I looked around the room and my eye caught the pink bra, hanging like a bright joke over our seriousness. When my eyes turned to Stephen I saw that he was looking at it too. He sat up straight and stretched out his legs and arms before breaking the silence.

'It's your turn now,' he said, looking at the vicar.

The vicar looked up and Stephen continued. 'Now you know my story. You know why I don't trust you. If you're so innocent, then tell us your story.' He nodded towards the bra. 'Tell us how that thing came to be in your study.'

The vicar's phone rang sharply and everybody jumped. He answered it.

'Yes, yes. That's OK. She's fine. Thank you for calling.'

He returned the phone to his pocket.

'Ambulance. They'll be fifteen minutes,' he whispered. 'Are you OK, Nollaig?'

'Yeah, I'm dead on, thanks.'

I'd almost forgotten about the ambulance. But it was on its way. Fifteen minutes of freedom left. Too short, too long. I just wanted it to be over. The vicar stood up straight.

'You're right, Stephen,' he said, 'I have been a coward. I will tell you my story. I very much hope that we can keep it between us ... But I suppose my time is up. I'm not a hypocrite, not really. Technically I haven't done anything wrong, but if it got out—'

'Just tell us,' I said. 'I'm about to be found out for faking my own death. How bad could your secret be?'

The vicar smiled and told us his story.

32

Stephen

He sat down on top of the table. You could see he was really starting to break. He looked old, somehow. Shoulders hunched over. Like he'd given up. Anyway, he began to speak and although I didn't really feel like listening I decided I'd try to keep my anger under control. The ambulance phoning had reminded me that Nollaig was the important one here. The last thing we needed was for her to go fainting again.

'The thing is, this . . . ' he waved his hand at the bra without looking at it, 'well, it's nothing really . . . nothing like what you think.'

I rolled my eyes but he ignored me and went on.

'I'll start from the start.' He took a breath. 'The first time I did it I was six and my mother caught me. She laughed. Not a horrible laugh. She was lovely, and she loved me every day until she died, even though she knew what I was, and she never told a soul.'

What he *was*? I gave Noll a raised-eyebrow look but she didn't see me. She was watching him really closely, listening to everything he said.

'I knew that it was something that little boys weren't meant to do, but also, in her laughter, I could hear that it was something that I would be allowed to do for a while at least. So I did. Not in front of my father, of course, because he was a religious man and a man's man too – not unkind, but very firm about the way that boys should behave.' He put on a deep, gruff voice. 'We should like rugby. We should have stern faces in trying situations, comfort the girls when they cried, hold doors open for them. We should have short haircuts and stiff upper lips.'

The vicar paused and his voice returned to normal. 'I didn't want to disappoint him, you see. So I kept it to myself. Mother only caught me once more, when I was sixteen. That was slightly more awkward. No laughter that time. I can still see her face and it pains me more than I can say, more than if she'd told Father, I expect. She didn't tell him, of course. What would she have said? *Gerald, darling, I've just found our son trying on my stockings.* No. She never spoke of it again, and neither did I. Not to anyone.'

My mouth fell open and I felt Nollaig sit up straight beside me. Wearing tights? Holy shit! But he didn't look at us, he just kept on.

'But I carried on doing it. You see, I was a boy. And now I am a man. But I was never a boy's boy, or a man's man, like my father. I knew that it was wrong, though. At least,' he seemed to struggle to find the right words, 'at least it felt right, but I knew that it wasn't meant to . . .'

I glanced at Noll and she had this big smirk on her face and she was biting her lip. Well, that was it, I couldn't keep a straight face then.

'Woah there, Vicar!' I waved my hand at him, giggling. 'What the hell are you saying?'

Nollaig snorted. I looked at her. Her face was creased up like she was in pain. She was trying not to laugh but it was too difficult.

'Oh my God . . . that bra?' she said, gasping for breath. 'That – that was *your* bra?'

We looked at each other and our faces totally broke up. Noll was covering her mouth with her hand. All this time we'd thought . . . and he . . . it was too much!

He didn't respond but his face was as pink as the lace on that bra. Holy shit.

'So, what?' I said. 'You're a tranny? You want to be a woman?'

'Do you wear high heels too, and make-up?' said Nollaig. 'Oh God. I'm sorry, I don't mean it in a bad way! But this is so random. Are you gay, then?'

'Gay?' I turned to her. 'I don't wear bras, do I?'

'No! I mean, well, I don't mean it in a bad way, but . . .' She was trying to hold her mouth straight but it kept turning up into a smile. 'Well, it's not exactly a *straight* thing to do, is it?'

Her face was full of laughter and, truth be told, I didn't know whether to be offended or find it hilarious. I could see her point, but I didn't like being reminded of the way that some people see me either. I was almost glad when the vicar broke in.

'No,' he said, quietly, 'I'm not gay. I have a wife, as you

know, and we're very happy. Well, we won't be if this gets out, of course . . . ' He was wringing his hands together nervously.

'Your wife doesn't know?' Nollaig stopped grinning.

'Nobody knows.'

Suddenly it didn't seem that funny any more. I remembered the picture of his family in his room and the voices of his kids calling in the hall when I'd gone round to his house that day. They'd get seriously mashed if people found out their vicar dad was a tranny. He spoke again, carefully, like he was trying to explain something complicated.

'And no, Stephen, I don't want to be a woman. When I was a child I knew that I was supposed to want to act like a man . . . but I couldn't. At least, not like the other men I knew. Not like my father, with his black leather prayer book and stiff suits and harsh aftershave that stung like fire. I was different, that's all.'

I could relate to that. But women's underwear? Fuck me . . . it really was something else. He carried on, starting to speak more quickly now as the words seemed to come more easily again.

'I didn't just join the ministry because I thought it might help me want to act like a man. I really felt called, you know . . . '

He was almost smiling as he talked about God and the Church. Nollaig, exhausted from the excitement, rested her head on my shoulder and we let him go on about it. The last thing I wanted to hear about was Jesus, but we were both tired.

'Each week my father would take me to church and we would face the front and listen to the sermon and stand for the hymns, my father would shush me when I fistled with sweet wrappers and when I turned my head he would put his big hand on top of it and turn it round again to face the front . . . '

He grinned like he was remembering something from a long time ago. You could see what he might have looked like as a kid when he smiled.

'But I couldn't help turning my head. The window at the back of the church. You know it – the one with the angel Gabriel telling Mary that she is to be the mother of Christ. I loved that picture.'

He had this wistful look on him as if he was in love or something, and instead of wringing his hands together he was waving them around now. He went on for what seemed like ages.

'When I speak to people during the service, I want them to hear the real me – not someone I'm pretending to be. The clothes? They're just a symbol of it. They make me feel more like myself. Does this make any sense?'

Noll and I nodded at the same time even though some of it didn't really make sense to me. We weren't laughing or even smiling any more, though. Somehow he made it seem real and the bra dangling from the picture frame was just a bra. I felt tired of it in a way and I wanted to take it down and put it back in the cupboard. But the vicar was still talking.

'I'd made this life for myself. This secret life, where underneath the garments of ministry I could wear the clothes of my true self. It was harming nobody. But if anyone found out! How much damage could have been done, then. The way that the world is . . . nobody would have understood.'

He looked at me. 'You're braver than me, Stephen. You faced Rob, and everything that that meant. You and your mum. You were very brave.'

He was right, but the mention of Mum brought me to

attention again. Something in my chest pulled away from him and towards myself and my family. I knew he was trying to be nice but I felt the tension in my stomach. I tried to keep it under control. He went on.

'I know that I should be more like you. Braver. But it's so hard. There's Alison, and the kids, and . . . '

I didn't want to like him but I felt Nollaig's hand touch mine and my fingers loosened and, despite wanting to hate him, I believed him. I knew that he meant it. And that would be enough for now. It would save me from punching his lights out, or telling the world what I knew about him, even if I felt like it. It was enough.

Then Nollaig did something that neither I nor the vicar expected. She got up, steadily, using the sofa to get herself to her feet and I jumped up to support her, and she said that she was OK, and she crossed the room to where the vicar was sitting on the table and she stood in front of him and stuck her left hand out and gestured for him to take it, and as he did she said, 'I'm sorry too,' and then turned around to me and offered me her other hand. I stepped forward and took it and we stood there in the dark room in this awkward chain of three, not really knowing what to say, until the pain came on Nollaig again and broke it.

33

Nollaig

Holy mother of fuck.

That's what it feels like. It feels like saying that, in a church. Shouting it. FUCK! But it's not a pain you can really describe because it's not a pain you are ever likely to have unless your body's doing what mine was doing: getting rid of a baby.

It's the kind of pain that makes you do things, makes you move. It brought me to my knees in that grotty little room. It pushed me to the ground and I cried out, and then it was gone again. Just like that.

'I . . . I'll phone the ambulance back.' The vicar fumbled about with his phone.

'Good idea. We should . . . we should probably start timing these or something,' said Stephen.

'What?' The vicar was punching numbers and shaking his phone as it rang, like that would make them pick up more quickly.

'It's what Mum was meant to do when Janie was born. You're meant to time how long they last, or maybe how long until the next one comes. Shit, I can't remember. Maybe it's in the book? Where is—'

'Sssssshh.' I squeezed Stephen's hand, hard. 'You're freaking me out. Calm down. I can't be having the baby now, it's too early.'

He shut up then but his eyes were wild, darting about, like he was looking for a solution. I tried not to feel the rising panic in the room but my heart was racing. It was too soon. It wasn't right to have these pains now. It wasn't normal. He brought me over to the sofa again. The book was sitting on the arm of it and he started flicking through it madly. What would he find in there? Unless there was a chapter called 'Everything's Going To Be Fine, Noll' then I didn't want to know. I didn't want to see any doctors. I didn't want the ambulance. I wanted everything to be normal and for this not to be happening. The vicar put his phone back into his pocket and told us they were five minutes away now. Not long.

'Ask me something,' I said. They both stared at me. I said it again. 'Ask me something.'

'Like what?' Stephen said, sitting beside me.

'Anything. I need to not think about all of this. Please, Stephen.' I could feel the tears coming. 'I want to talk about something, anything, except ambulances and hospitals.'

'Sssssshh, OK, OK.' He was whispering his words and rubbing my hand, too hard.

'I have a question, Nollaig,' the vicar said.

We both looked up. He was sitting on his spot on the table again. I nodded and he spoke in a matter-of-fact tone.

'It's nosey of me, I know. But I think you know that you can trust me now.' He offered a weak, hopeful smile. 'I thought, assumed, that Stephen was your boyfriend.' Stephen smirked. 'But, now I know that he obviously isn't. So I was wondering . . . Who is the father of your baby, Nollaig?'

'She said she didn't want to talk about the baby, dimwit,' Stephen scowled.

'No, wait,' I said, turning to Stephen, 'I didn't say that. I said I didn't want to talk about hospitals.'

'What?' he turned to me, incredulous. 'I asked you who the da was and you wouldn't say! Are you seriously gonna tell *him*?'

A twinge in my side. Oof. Stephen's anger melted into concern and he squeezed my hand hard.

'Are you OK? Is it another contraction?'

'It's OK, I'm OK,' I said, taking a breath. 'The baby just whacked me in the side. Don't think she's keen to stay in here for much longer.' I tried to smile but I was getting tired. 'Stephen, I'm sorry I didn't tell you. I wanted to. I really did. But, I suppose I just hoped that if I didn't tell anyone then it wouldn't be true . . .'

'And you don't mind talking about it now?'

It was hard for him to understand, I could see that. It was hard to explain, though. He was going to freak out. I wished that I had a different truth to tell, but I didn't. I couldn't undo anything.

'No,' I looked at him, 'I have to tell you now.'

And I leant back on the lumpy sofa and closed my eyes and told my best friend and a vicar I hardly knew about the best and worst moment of my life.

'It was during the summer. You were away, Stephen.'

'In Dublin, with Mum and Janie.'

'Yes.'

Loads of families go away on holiday over the Twelfth of July fortnight here. It's a good way to avoid the hassle of roads being blocked because of the Loyalist marches, or for some people it's an excuse not to join in if they don't want to. Stephen's mum took him away because she was terrified of him getting into trouble, which he thought was stupid, because he wasn't interested in bands or flag waving, but I secretly thought she had a point. Those kids that made a big thing out of being one religion or another really wound him up.

'So, you were away. It was the eleventh, and I was out at the shops getting bread and stuff, and I bumped into Kyle Freeman in Tesco.'

'Kyle? Kyle Freeman?!'

'Sssshh. It's not him. I just bumped into him. Let me tell the thing. Kyle smiled at me and said hello. It must have shocked me because he laughed then and said something about how he wasn't gonna bite me. I smiled back and said hello too. And then he did something that nobody had ever done before. He invited me to a party.'

'You went to a party and never told me about it?'

'Stephen,' pleaded the vicar. 'Let her talk.'

'Yes, I went to a party. I wouldn't have if he hadn't smiled at me. But I was curious. And bored. And Dad was being a dick as usual. So I went.'

'And? What happened?'

'Well, I got there and everyone was already pissed. A couple of people burst out laughing when I walked in but it didn't bother me.'

It did bother me, a bit. I mean, I never wanted to be like them. But I did wonder what it must be like to not have everyone staring at you all the time, thinking how much of a freak you were, afraid of you. If only I'd known how much worse things could get. A split second decision. One of those 'Oh what the hell?' moments where you know a thing isn't a good idea but you do it anyway. I'd gone over it again and again. If only I'd been in a better mood, I might not have bothered going to that party in the first place. It was Dad's fault really. I'd made him beans on toast and he said I'd burnt the toast. I hadn't – he was just picking a fight – but he was low on booze and I should've known not to say anything.

'It's not burnt.'

That was all. I didn't say anything else. He threw the bloody toaster right at my head and as I ran out I could hear him smashing other stuff up as well. Fuck it, I thought, I'll get myself some stuff in Tesco and have it in the park and go home when he's passed out. I hated him, hated having to look after him, hated not having a place I could be indoors. I fumed my way around the aisles at Tesco until I bumped into Kyle and then my plans changed. My whole life changed. I went to the stupid party because why not? Why not do something different?

I continued talking.

'So anyway, I was gonna just leave again, and I was turning around when he came over.'

'Who?'

I looked at Stephen, leaning in as if he didn't want to miss a word. My best friend. The one who had helped me every day for weeks now. Months, years even. I didn't want to tell him but now was the right moment.

'Craig McRoberts.'

His mouth fell open. He didn't speak.

'I didn't really want to. I didn't actually ever like him.'

I didn't like him that night either. He would never be the kind of guy I'd like, even if he was a nicer person. He liked designer clothes and his hair was short and too neat and he was wearing expensive smelling aftershave that made me want to retch.

The vicar cut in, concern in his voice, 'Nollaig, this boy, Craig.' I felt Stephen wince at his name. 'Did he ... did he force you?'

'What? No. No, he didn't. Jesus. He's a wee shite but he didn't do that.'

He had come over, half cut, and shoved a can of lager into my hand.

''Mon, Noll! It's not a party if yer not getting trashed!'

I took the can and he grabbed my hand and pulled me into the middle of the room, a can and a fag both in his other hand. Dead cool. Urgh. So much for my plan to go and have a drink quietly and watch people. There I was, standing in the middle of someone's living room, face beaming.

'Ach now, don't be shy, Nollaig!' He danced around me. The music was banging, the bass louder than the tune, I felt it in my chest. 'Have a wee dance!' I took a drink. And another. Nobody was really paying attention anyway. Maybe this was how to be normal – have a drink, pretend it was a laugh, you could always say you were pissed the next day. That's what people did, right?

I tried to blink away the detail. The crap music beating in my head, the choking fag smoke, Craig getting closer, pulling me to his chest.

'It was only once. I didn't really like him,' I said to Stephen.

He just sat there, looking at me in silence. Craig was the one who tormented him. The one whose rich da got him out of every scrape, every detention.

'I'd had a few drinks cos I was annoyed with Dad, and I felt sick the whole time. It was horrible and I hated myself after, and then, and then I had to go home and it was late and Dad was pissed and . . .'

I broke down then. I remembered. Craig McRoberts. He was all over me, and in a way it felt good as well as horrible. Fuck it, I thought, why not? I led him out of the room and up the stairs, downing another can on the way, trying not to think about anything, so sick of thinking, the freezing bedroom, his hands on me, under my t-shirt, that moment when I wished I hadn't started it but I didn't want to stop it either, his breath that smelled of stale lager and fag ash, panting in my face, making me want to throw up. Stumbling home, crying. Dad, whacking me round the head and then him crying and asking me to forgive him. And now, knowing that I was going to be a shit mum and that Craig McRoberts's rich family would have to know about it and they'd probably make me give my baby away so they didn't have to live with the shame of it being brought up by a wee slag like me.

The vicar came over and sat on my other side. He put an awkward arm around me and I was glad of it. I sobbed into his big knitted jumper and we sat there for a while and then his phone rang and the three of us all jumped in unison. The vicar grabbed it and answered. The ambulance had arrived.

The paramedics were so fast once they'd found us. There wasn't time to be afraid. They were bundling me onto a stretcher, fiddling with blood pressure cuffs and straps and asking me a string of questions: How many weeks pregnant was I? Had there been any bleeding? Was there any pain? Which hospital was I registered with?

They raised an eyebrow at the vicar when I said I hadn't been to see a doctor yet. The vicar shrugged and I suddenly realised what the paramedics were thinking. Surely it would be OK, though? We could tell them what had happened. Stephen could explain. Stephen. Where was he? I lifted my shoulders up off the stretcher to try and look around but the paramedic pushed me gently back down again. 'It's important for you to keep still now, Nollaig.' They started lifting me up the stairs towards the crypt door. I could only see the ceiling, and then the sky. It was getting dark and starting to snow again.

'Brian!' It was the first time I had used his name. It sounded weird in my mouth and I almost laughed as the tears stung my face.

'I'm here, Nollaig.'

'Where's Stephen?'

'Is Stephen the baby's dad?' asked the paramedic.

I ignored him.

'Where is he?'

'I'm sorry, Nollaig,' the vicar said, 'he left as soon as the ambulance arrived.'

34

Stephen

As I slipped out of the crypt and up the stairs, my head was full of all these thoughts that were trying to punch each other's lights out:

Nollaig was never my friend.

Nollaig was the best friend I ever had and now I'm leaving her.

I want to kill Craig McRoberts for doing that to her.

But he's the dad of her baby, I'd be killing the dad of her baby.

I couldn't get my head around it. As I passed the window I glanced up at the angel telling Mary a whole bunch of stuff she probably didn't want to hear. I gave the pair of them the fingers and started running. I ran past the toppled Christmas tree, out of the church into the falling snow and down the street. Past all the people who didn't know that my life was breaking apart, towards my home.

I knew I was going to have to tell my mum something that would make her hate me. It wasn't fair and I didn't really know who to blame for it all – Nollaig, Craig, the vicar. Maybe it was me that was to blame. Maybe I should have just told Mum in the first place. After all, she was the only person in my life that stuck by me, wasn't she?

I slowed down, gasping, the freezing air pounding in my lungs. Why Craig? Of all people. It was only once, but still. I trudged through the puddles of slush. Nearly home now. Christmas tree lights, strung up across the street, were twinkling on and off and I couldn't remember when they'd gone up. I hated Craig. I hated him so much. Nollaig was going to be tied to him forever now. My stomach lurched and I coughed and threw up at the side of the road. An old lady walking her dog went by and tutted. I wished that I had someone to talk to but the only person that I could think of was Nollaig.

I approached our door and I could see the TV flickering in the window and Janie bouncing on the sofa watching her cartoons. It always looked so warm, our house. When you went round to Nollaig's it never looked like that. It was mostly always dark, and even when the lights were on it seemed so quiet and lonely. I was so nervous that I almost knocked on my own door, like a stranger.

Mum was in the kitchen having a cup of tea and reading a book. There were dirty dishes everywhere and her hair was wrapped up in a towel.

'Hiya love, fancy a takeaway for tea? I'm knackered after that service.'

I sat down opposite her, and spoke.

'Mum. I have something to tell you. Something really big.'

She put her book down and her faced dropped.

'OK. Is it something bad? Are you in trouble with the cops?'

'No. I mean, it's bad in a way ...' I looked up at her. She was sitting really still, like if she made a movement something might break. 'It's bad because ... because I told you a lie.'

'OK.' She took a breath. 'OK. Just tell me then. What is it?'

Janie burst in the door and ran over to Mum. Mum tried to smile at her and pulled her up onto her knee. 'Mummy needs to talk to Stevie now, love. Will you go back and watch your cartoons?' Janie shook her head, no.

'It's OK, she can stay,' I said.

'No. She cannot,' said Mum, standing up and carrying Janie to the door. Janie started to cry and Mum lifted a digestive biscuit and handed it to her as they left the room. Mum returned and sat down opposite me again.

'OK.' Her face was stern. 'We have the time it takes for that biscuit to get eaten. Spit it out.'

'Nollaig's alive.'

Her eyes widened and she put a hand to her chest.

'Jesus Christ. What?'

'I'm sorry, Mum. She's not dead. And I know I should have told you. I know I should have. But she's in big trouble.'

'Oh my God, I can't believe it ...' She was half laughing but her hand was still on her chest. 'But we ... we went to church today ... and ... I was, and you ... Hang on. Did you know? Did you know when we were in church today that she was alive?'

235

The room was silent for a moment. Mum was shaking her head and staring at me. Her voice went higher.

'You did the flowers for the church, Stephen.' Tears sprang to her eyes. 'You did the fucking flowers.'

'I know. I know. I'm so sorry, Mum. I didn't know what to do. She's really in trouble.'

'She's not the only one.' But she said it quietly as fat tears rolled down her face. My stomach cramped up. Nollaig, the vicar, me; we'd all lied.

'I'm really, really sorry, Mum.'

And I *was* sorry. She'd stuck up for me all these years and how had I repaid her? She'd never get over this one, never. It was much worse than I thought it was going to be. She wasn't even going to get mad. I had broken her. I looked at the floor, unable to bear the pain in her face. The tap dripped and I could hear Janie giggling at her cartoons.

'Oh, fuck it,' Mum said.

I looked up. She was standing up with her hands on the table. She wiped her eyes and looked directly at me.

'Tell me everything. Come on, you might as well. Tell me the whole bloody thing and what about this trouble she's in? Don't you bloody leave anything out this time, Stephen, I want to know the lot. That girl's worse off than anyone in this house and if she's in trouble then we're going to help her.'

I couldn't believe it.

'Don't give me that look. I've been through worse than having you tell me a lie, son. Don't forget that.' She took the towel off her head and pushed her hair behind her ears.

'What makes a fifteen-year-old fake her own death? That's

236

what I want to know. If she's in the kind of trouble I was in then she's gonna need us all. Tell me the whole thing. Now. Before our Janie finishes that bloody digestive biscuit.'

She was still standing up. I shrank before her but my heart swelled inside my chest. This was a battle, and she was on my side, and I was on Nollaig's side, and we were going to fight.

35

Nollaig

I hadn't really been in a hospital before, not that I remembered anyway. When Mum was really ill they kept me away from her. I don't know why. Maybe they thought I'd be scared. But I felt too tired to be scared. At least now I didn't have to keep looking at that book. It wasn't all up to me any more. The first thing they did was give me a scan. I watched the dark little human thing moving on the screen. Hello, I thought, can you hear my thoughts? Do they travel from my brain into yours, the way that my blood does? The way that my life does? And the doctor's voice got further and further away as I sent my brain's thoughts to my baby, implanting ideas and pictures and good words that she might be born with: you are good; I will always love you; stand up for yourself; be strong; be better than me.

Brian was standing at the side of the bed, chatting to the doctor. He'd told them that he found me hiding in the church on the day of the service. It wasn't a total lie. He just didn't mention that it wasn't the first time that he found me there. I wasn't going to say any different. He had brought me here and I hadn't wanted to come, and I knew that things were going to change and that maybe . . . but I couldn't think of it. I wasn't going to think about it. For as long as she was inside me I would try to imagine goodness and being strong, and maybe in the future she would remember this connection. Nobody could unconnect us or separate our blood, could they? She'd always be mine.

And as I lay there thinking about our connection I must have drifted into sleep, and the bed became the back of an angel, and we lay on its silky white dress flying high above the hospital. The angel's wings waved gently and the warm air rolled over us and nobody below could even see where we were.

When I woke up the doctor was gone and there were five people sitting beside me. I didn't recognise one of them. She was standing beside Brian. Stephen and Stephen's mum were on the other side. Stephen's mum was holding Janic. I tried to speak but she put her finger to her lips.

'Sssshh, just relax, Nollaig.' She smiled.

Maybe I was still dreaming. Why wasn't she angry? Why was Stephen here? After everything I'd done to him.

'Don't look so worried, Noll,' Stephen said. He was holding a bunch of grapes and shoving them into his mouth as he spoke. 'Brought you these. But I'm starving. I'll get you some more, OK? He grinned and I smiled back at him.

'I'm glad you're here,' I whispered.

'Me too.' He looked at his mum and turned back to me, with a serious look. 'Noll, Mum knows everything now. I had to tell her.'

'Everything?' I glanced at Brian who looked at his feet.

'Yes, love,' said Stephen's mum. She looked at me and then at the vicar, offering him a half smile.

'That's OK,' I whispered again. I was feeling more awake now. I looked at the stranger standing beside Brian.

'Are you his wife?' I asked the woman. Everybody laughed and Brian went red.

'In his dreams, love!' the woman said and everyone laughed again. She was short and fat with cropped red hair, a purple scarf wound round her neck and bright purple earrings. I remembered the woman from the photo in Brian's room in the church. Nothing like her at all.

'Naw, love, I'm Geraldine, your social worker.'

'I didn't know I had a social worker.'

'You didn't!' she said with a smile. 'But you do now. We'll have a little talk when your visitors have gone.'

'I don't want them to leave!'

'It's OK, Nollaig,' said Brian, putting a hand on my arm, just below the blood pressure cuff. 'You can trust Geraldine. She wants to help you.'

'You're safe now,' said Geraldine.

Yeah right. If I could have got out of that bed and run away that instant I would have. But I had all sorts of crap tying me to the bed: the blood pressure thing, and another machine that was bleeping and flashing. Not to mention the five of them gawking at me. I closed my eyes to make them disappear for a minute.

'Do you want us to leave, Noll?' said Stephen.

I opened an eye. 'Will you stay? Just you, I mean?' I asked.

They all looked at one another and shuffled off, leaving me alone with Stephen. When they were gone he pulled the big curtain around my bed.

'I don't think you're meant to do that,' I said. 'I think it's only nurses that do that.'

He grinned as he sat on the edge of my bed.

'I think that getting into shit with the nurses is the least of our worries.'

He was right. What a mess. And all because of me.

'Hey,' he squeezed my arm, 'don't look so miserable. It's not that bad.'

'You don't hate me then?'

He smirked. 'Nobody's perfect, right? And who would I watch Jeremy Kyle with if you weren't around?'

I smiled weakly. I knew he was trying to say the right thing. How could he really forgive me for being with Craig? The thought made me want to throw up.

'You OK? You look like you're gonna boke. Do you want one of those wee cardboard bowls?' He lifted one from beside the bed and handed it to me. 'They're dead wee, aren't they? What if you really need to chunder?'

I giggled. 'I'm OK. Just thinking about the baby's dad.'

For some reason that made us both crack up. It wasn't funny, but somehow it was. Stephen popped another grape into his mouth and offered me one. I shuffled myself to a more upright position and took one, cracking the cold skin of it between my teeth. It was so sweet.

'Noll. There's a chance, just a chance, that my mum will be able to help you out.'

He was trying not to show it but his eyes were gleaming with excitement.

'What do you mean?'

'Well. She's asked that woman – the social worker woman – about letting you stay with us for a bit.'

'What? What do you mean? Does she ... does she know about Dad?'

'Yeah, I told Mum that he hit you.' He popped another grape, like it was nothing serious. 'I hope that's OK, but I didn't really have a choice.'

He offered me the grapes and I took a couple. My head was starting to spin.

'So anyway,' he went on, 'Mum told the social worker, just about an hour ago. You were sleeping. And she asked her if you could stay with us instead of getting fostered or whatever.'

I swallowed my grape. My heart started to race.

'She'd do that? For me? Oh my God, Stephen, that would be amazing of her. I'd go to school, and everything, and I'd be dead quiet, she'd not even know that I was there, and—'

'Look,' he grew serious, 'I don't know if it's possible or not yet. The social worker's gonna talk to you about it. But it might work out. I hope it does too. But if it doesn't ... If it doesn't then we'll stick together, OK? Whatever happens. We'll still be friends, OK?'

I knew it was a slim chance. And beyond the hope there was the creeping guilt. I knew that Steve's mum was up to her eyes with Janie and Stephen. Her house was a mess and they didn't have a spare room – where the hell would I even sleep? And wasn't she angry with Stephen about him lying to her? I couldn't believe she was being so generous. The fact that she had even thought about it was making my brain buzz. Why would anyone be that kind?

'I can't really believe it, though,' I said. 'It's so nice of her ...'

'I know,' said Stephen. 'I should have known she'd be like that, though. She hates bullies as much as you do, Nollaig. You're quite like her really.'

'What about Brian? Does she know ... about him? What did she say?'

'I thought she'd go nuts,' Stephen said, popping another grape. 'But it turns out she had this friend since school who dresses up too.'

'Fuck off!'

'No, seriously. It didn't faze her. She was raging about the blackmail, though.'

'Shit ...'

'I know. Grounded for life ...' He didn't look too worried, munching grapes on the bed.

'Stephen. When I was in the church ... the angel ...'

'The one in the window? What about it?'

'Did you ever ... och, it doesn't matter. It's stupid.'

Everything in the church seemed miles away now. I was sure I'd imagined lots of things.

'No. It isn't,' he said. 'That window was a bit weird, wasn't it?'

'Yeah. Weird. But in a good way.'

'I know what you mean.'

The curtain was whisked back and a nurse scowled at Stephen. He grinned back at her cheekily and winked at me before hopping off the bed.

'You can have these,' he said, throwing the grapes onto my lap. 'I'll get the social worker to come in now, OK?'

'OK!' I said.

He left and I watched the ward door swing open to reveal them standing in a loose huddle: Stephen's mum with Janie, asleep in her arms; Geraldine, the social worker, her bright hair glowing in the harsh hospital lights; and Brian, the vicar, sipping tea from a plastic cup and looking up to offer Stephen his hand as the door swung back. I stared at the ceiling and put my hands on my belly and breathed slowly, in and out.

Dear Lord,

Hello. It's me, Veronica. I'm still the same person. It's just me, in a dress. But you know that. You always knew that, perhaps even better than I did myself. And now some other people know as well. Not many, but enough for now, I think.

Anyway, I'm here for two reasons and the first is a request, for Nollaig. I promised her I would put in a word for her this morning and so here I am. She and baby Maria are doing splendidly but she does worry. I suppose that anyone who had such a long stay in hospital while pregnant might feel the same, and perhaps particularly someone so young. May her faith in herself as a mother grow with every moment of the lovely little Maria's development.

I want to pray also for Stephen and his mum. They have been such wonderful friends to Nollaig and I know it can't be easy for them all squashed into that little house, and yet when I visit I can see that they are happy in the chaos. It is a warm house. Just right for children. Help me to remember them – to notice their needs.

And that is the other reason that I'm here, Lord. To talk about needs. You see, I thought I was helping Nollaig and

Stephen, but really they were helping me. I was never going to tell Alison without a little push, was I? In the end, though, they didn't force me. Nobody did. I told her myself, because it was time and because I wanted to. I looked at Nollaig in her hospital bed that night and I watched her watching the heartbeat monitors – hers and her baby's – and I thought, I have two hearts as well. And it is so terrifying to think of both of them being broken. But if this girl who has nothing, not even a home, could lie there and look real life in the face, then perhaps I could too. So I went home and I told Alison all about Veronica.

I told her everything. She cried. And I thought it was all over. But they were tears of relief. She had thought I'd been having an affair, just like Stephen and Nollaig had. All the sneaking around and things going missing. I had been so careful to keep all of the evidence out of the house. But I suppose you can't hide how you look when you're so miserable, or how you feel when you've been out finding your freedom. She knew it was someone else. She just didn't realise that the someone else was me. And it is me, Lord. I haven't changed. I'm just letting myself be more of myself. And it feels . . . strange. And good. And things will be a bit strange between me and Alison for a while, I think. But I think they will be good, eventually. And so I end this prayer with a word of thanks, because you did help me after all.

Thank you.

Amen.

KM.

JOIN US ONLINE

FOR THE LATEST NEWS, REVIEWS AND SHINY NEW BOOKS FROM THE WORLD OF

ATOM

Sign up to

the Journal

at

http://bit.ly/AtomTheJournal

🐦 @AtomBooks

f /AtomBooks

📷 @atombooks

🎧 atombooks

WWW.ATOMBOOKS.CO.UK